Zora and Me

The Summoner

ZORA AND ME

THE SUMMONER

VICTORIA BOND

CANDLEWICK PRESS

Copyright © 2020 by Victoria Bond

First edition 2020

Library of Congress Catalog Card Number pending
ISBN 978-0-7636-4299-0 (hardcover)
ISBN 978-1-5362-1667-7 (paperback)

20 21 22 23 24 25 LBM 10 9 8 7 6 5 4 3 2 1

Printed in Melrose Park, IL, USA

This book was typeset in Centaur MT.

Candlewick Press
99 Dover Street
Somerville, Massachusetts 02144

www.candlewick.com

For my son, Keats Merritt Bond Baughman.
You are my needle pointing north.

Eatonville, Florida
September 29, 1956

Granddaughter:

Every day since I was fourteen, the scar on my left hand reminds me of your grandfather, my dear Teddy. He told me that the scar would fade, and he was right—it mostly did. But when I hold my hand up in the bright noonday light, a shadow of that 1905 scar survives.

Everyone in Eatonville suffered terribly that year, including my best friend, Zora. Grief and loss afflicted us both. It chased us through a grove in the lightning and rain. At kitchen tables and on porch swings, at swamp banks and in dark cabins, loss bore down on our necks with icy blue and stinging breath. The faded scar on my hand is a testament to how Teddy and Eatonville helped me to heal in place. They were my anchors, my salve, my proof of miracles.

Grief prodded Zora to reject miracles. She insisted, instead, that earth and life on it make sense. Stories are the thing that anchored her. Eatonville itself couldn't give her peace, but *stories* about Eatonville might.

She carried the story of Eatonville with her around the world. Stories protected her, healed her. And the summer of 1905 was Zora's last in Eatonville.

And now you, her namesake, are leaving. I offer the story of our parting as a goodbye. I hope this story will be for you a harbor in the storm.

The final thing I must say is: fear no loss. Despite our efforts, loss touches us all. Stand brave, dear girl. Loss will not be your undoing. Loss cannot hold a candle to love. Love is our story.

Your grandmother,
Carrie Baker

PART ONE

CHAPTER ONE

Mama's employers, the Brays, had gone on summer vacation to the South Carolina shore. Usually, when the Brays went away, Mama looked after Mrs. Bray's old aunt, Miss Pitty. But in the summer of 1905, Mama had somehow convinced Mrs. Bray to take the elderly Miss Pitty along with them. It was the very first vacation she had ever been granted in a lifetime of labor. Triumphant, Mama declared her intention to keep right on working full days, but with me. Working with me, working for *us*, was different.

It's almost hard to believe now that I was just thirteen when I started taking in laundry from Lake

Maitland. A couple days a week, I boiled water in a zinc barrel and dropped tablecloths and sheets in with the lye soap I made. I stirred, I rinsed, I wrung. Then I hung the large white squares on the line alongside our house. On hot days, I stewed in stifling tedium. On windy days, the linens billowed like clouds and the sight gave me pride in my work.

With Mama's help that summer, I could complete twice the loads in half the time. I was able to earn more, too, with leftover time for relaxing. Instead of unpinning sheets from the line and ironing in the early evening, I could sit beside Mama on our porch swing, cross-stitch, and watch the deepening sky coax out the first stars. That summer, Mama's oval face glowed with health and peace. I remember feeling the only way you can after spending a perfectly sorted day doing good and honest work beside someone you love: grateful.

On one such evening, the sound of an engine and a small black cloud announced the speedy approach of a horseless carriage. We squinted into the setting sun to make out who it was.

"It's Mr. Baker," Mama said. I stood, overjoyed, certain that Teddy would be with him. Teddy hadn't mentioned dropping by. No matter. Whether he appeared at my door, we met at the Loving Pine, we crossed paths in the forest where there were no paths, or we bumped into each other on Joe Clarke's porch, where it felt like all paths led, Teddy, in my heart and in my home, was always welcome and always new. Teddy waved from the front seat, beside his father.

The horseless drew very close now. Mr. Baker parked it next to a spiky, squat palm in our yard and killed the engine. There was another surprise! Zora was riding in the back.

"Hello there," Mr. Baker called, his silver spectacles catching the light. His friendly, routine words were one thing, his tone another. He sounded as if he were trying to keep down a roaring cough, stifle something. Teddy got out of the automobile in a hurry, but Zora still managed to beat him to the dooryard. They were both electric with some sort of news. I couldn't tell if it was bad news, exciting news, or both.

Mama picked up on it, too, and got straight to the point. "Alan, what's going on?"

Mr. Baker took off his hat. "A white law man came to Joe Clarke's today," he said cheerlessly, "a sheriff from Sanford."

"What about?" There was dread in her voice.

"There's a man on the run by the name of Terrace

Side," Mr. Baker said. "This white sheriff says this Mr. Side escaped from a chain gang stationed in Georgia, at the border. The authorities suspect the fugitive's trekking all night and hiding out all day. They even suspect he's heading to Eatonville, for refuge."

"Why?" Mama asked. "Does he have people in Eatonville? Ain't no one here called Side, is there?"

"No, ma'am," Mr. Baker answered. "But that sheriff thinks Side would come here, counting on the protection of something more formidable than a single colored family: an entire colored town." Mr. Baker paused. "You know what Joe Clarke told that white man to his face?" he asked, a small grim smile on his lips. "He said, *Eatonville doesn't harbor murderers, black or white.*"

"That's just what Mr. Clarke told him," Teddy said, awe and respect in his voice and expression.

"So is that what this Side fellow got put away for, murder?" Mama was more businesslike than impressed.

"Yes," Mr. Baker answered, "according to that sheriff."

"But do we know for sure?" While I reeled, Mama's common sense raged. "For all we know, he might have knocked over a houseplant in some rich white lady's house. For all we know, this man may be guilty only of running for his life."

"We don't know," Mr. Baker said, somber and defeated-like. "The one thing we know for sure is that the white law man says anyone who dares to abet the fugitive will be punished, severely. Search parties from Georgia will be coming through, looking for Side's hideout. So we've got to get the word out to everyone, including folks in Blue Bay and Lake Catherine. Keep your door and windows locked, a lantern lit," Mr. Baker advised. "A house with the lights on won't look like a good hiding place to either a fugitive or a mob." Mr. Baker looked at Teddy. "We better get on. We've got the ride of Paul Revere ahead of us and still got Zora here to drop home."

An awkward silence followed.

John Hurston was on the road and had been for weeks, traveling the borders of Alabama, Georgia, and Florida on a preaching tour. Lucy Hurston had been taking to her bed on and off since he'd gone. More than ever, Zora was needed at home.

"This is all precaution," Mr. Baker tried to reassure. "That's all, precaution. I'm not sure that Side man is here in Eatonville. The poor man may very well be apprehended even before the search parties get here." Mr. Baker shook his head. "Heaven help him if he is."

"I'm no martyr, so I'm not going out looking for Side tonight," said Mama, "but if Side finds his way to my house seeking refuge, it's my Christian duty to help him."

Teddy blinked, rocked back on his heels by my mother's bravery. Zora got incredibly still. In admiration, I think, for Mama's Christian virtue. My lips quivered. Mr. Baker pursed his. "Be careful," he cautioned, "very, very careful."

"I will," Mama answered quietly, "by putting my faith in the Lord. Tonight, I'll be praying for everybody in Eatonville, *everybody*."

CHAPTER TWO

After a late supper, we set our hands, if not our minds, to sewing and needlework at our table. Mama worked on trimming the collar of a blouse with a lace wreath. I returned to my cross-stitch of a lamb beneath the crucifix. Earlier I had made such little progress on the rugged cross that I abandoned it altogether to work on the lamb's ebony eyes. As I threaded a new needle with black thread, we were startled by howls, barks, and the trampling of feet in our dooryard.

In one fluid motion, Mama rose from her chair, grabbed me, and shoved me under the table. Staying on her hands and knees, she crawled over to the

front window and crouched below it. The porch
swing chain jangled and shrieked and whined. Dogs
scratched wildly at the door. Fists pounded at it. The
butt of a gun hammered at it. The hinges rattled. My
bowels tightened.

"Open up!" a voice ripped the night. "Open up!"
The dogs quieted and the swift response to an order
of any kind indicated there were fewer animals than I
feared, probably no more than three, but it only took
one dog to maim, kill. Who were these people who
had come with dogs? Why were they here?

"I live here," Mama called, her voice steady.
"This is my house." Mama and I locked eyes. Hers
instructed me to remain silent.

The butt of a gun hammered again, hard. "Fugitive
search! Open up! Now!" Mama jumped up and sprang
the door ajar.

Two dogs, three men. The man with the rifle
stepped into our home. One of the dogs came with
him. One look and I knew I couldn't maroon my
mother. I crawled out from under the table and hurried over to stand beside her.

"That's right," the man said, his tidewater-green
eyes appraising us. The dog sniffed around our meager sitting room, put its paws on our table and our

sewing, then dashed off to our bedroom. The animal was searching for the scent it had been trained to find: Terrace Side.

"Why are you here?" Mama asked.

The man went to our table and rubbed a dirty thumb over the paw print left on my cross-stitch by the dog, deepening the stain. The kitchen clock ticked slowly, loudly. "We're looking for something. My dog Pixie will tell us if that something happens to be here."

One of the other two men also stepped inside. A wide-brimmed hat made his neck look thick. The third kept watch on the porch with the other dog. Pixie came out of our bedroom and returned to her master's side.

The man rubbed the dog's fawn-colored fur affectionately. "Pixie say no one else here. Pixie say you all alone—till we got here, anyway. I can't believe that, the two of you, much prettier than them fancy ribbons and lace. Much prettier," he nattered on. "And you all alone."

Tidewater Eyes reached out and laid his filthy hand on my mother's neck. Thick Neck lifted the brim of his hat to better observe his friend's actions.

I held my breath. Mama gritted her teeth. I

feared this man's touch was going to choke us both. "Sir"—fear and disgust stretched Mama's lips into a grimace—"if your business here is done, please leave us be." Then she prayed. "Please, Lord, please. Instruct these men to leave us be."

God answered, with a solution the devil could cotton to. Out on the road, an engine snarled and a horn tooted shrilly.

Then a monstrously musical voice beckoned: *"The nigger's been caught! Come on, fellas! Come on outta there! Let's go have us some real fun! Yahoo! Bells are a-ringing! Bells are a-ringing! The nigger's been caught at Lake Bell! Let's go have some real fun! At Lake Bell! Yahoo! The nigger's been caught at Lake Bell. Bells are a-ringing!"*

Two women alone in a house were a mere sideshow. The torture of Terrace Side was the main event. The man and the dog on the porch went to join the troop down on the road. Thick Neck also withdrew. Tidewater Eyes removed his hand from Mama's neck. I quickly grabbed her wrist, in order to subdue her urge to spit in his face.

"We've got to go," he said, almost as if he were apologizing. "But would you first be so kind as to answer a question for me?"

He didn't bother to wait for Mama's answer.

"How far is Lake Bell from here?"

Mama admitted what could not be disputed: "Not far."

"Not far as in the next town over, or not far as in right here in your little colored part of this country?"

Mama was silent.

"Ah," he said. "Looks like Eatonville is a winner!"

The horseless rattled to life, and Tidewater left, Pixie trotting beside him.

Hell moved on in a pack. It had less than a quarter mile to go before arriving at Lake Bell.

Mama stood limp by our table. I staggered over to close the front door and then retched. The gesture shattered the veneer of my anger. Raw pain at our vulnerability writhed beneath it. Finally, Mama and I collapsed and wept, clinging to each other as if to rafts in a flood.

We didn't know Terrace Side, had never laid eyes on him. Yet he had delivered to us a near-catastrophe.

CHAPTER THREE

N ear dawn, we finally slept. When we woke at midmorning, Mama and I dressed and went immediately to the Hurstons' to check on them. Everywhere the air was smoky, putrid, gray. The mob had set a fire; that much was sure. Sadly, I prayed that if Terrace Side had died, he had done so alone, that no one from Eatonville had suffered alongside him.

The shadows of the chinaberry leaves flickered on the Hurstons' roof. Lucy Hurston sat on the porch in the tall rocker: a papery blossom, hardly occupying a sliver of shade.

On seeing how Mrs. Hurston looked, Mama dashed up the path ahead of me. "Lucy Hurston!" Mama scolded. "You should be in bed! Why you out? Why?"

Lucy Hurston smiled weakly. "I feel better than I look, and that's saying something at a time like this." She slid on her cotton corded slippers and made to stand, using the arms of the chair for support. Mama went to steady her, but Lucy Hurston held her own.

"Old Lady Bronson's lemon-and-onion syrup would do you some good," Mama declared. "And with all those pills Doc Brazzle rolls, he sure enough must have something that will help you rest, sleep."

Zora came out on the porch. Mrs. Hurston grabbed her daughter's hand. "Who could sleep with what went on in this town last night?" Lucy Hurston asked. "Tell me, did you sleep?"

"Barely," Mama answered. "We had unexpected visitors."

Zora reached out to me tenderly, but I involuntarily flinched. The shock at what my reflex intimated caused her to throw her hand to her mouth. I had surprised even myself. Contritely, I took her hand and placed it over my heart, my way of reassuring her. The realization startled Lucy Hurston. Mama shook her head and said, "No, not that, thankfully."

"Are you all right?" Lucy Hurston asked softly. "You really both all right?"

"Yes," I answered.

Zora exhaled. "The mob rode past here. We heard them. That was all. That was enough."

"Side was discovered at Lake Bell," Mama said. "The men that came to our place went with a gang there—" And Lucy Hurston shivered with the knowledge of what the mob went *there* to do, how men with their guns cocked and torches alight could set foot anywhere—on our shores, our land, our doorstep—and assume ownership of all our property, including our bodies and souls.

Mama said, "Let me take you inside, Lucy. You should be lying down." Mrs. Hurston obliged, and the two disappeared inside the house.

Ever since Lucy Hurston had returned home from Alabama, she'd been bad and then worse.

Her youngest sister had birthed a baby boy two months before it was his time to come. A letter arrived detailing how the first-time mother had lost a pitcher of blood, the baby no bigger than a pine cone. Immediately, Mrs. Hurston set out for Notasulga,

Alabama, by train to be with her sister and tiny nephew. Neither survived.

While Mrs. Hurston was in Alabama, John Hurston began what was to be his last preaching tour. It was Lucy Hurston who had pushed the idea of it being his last time out on the road. At first, John Hurston resisted. Lucy Hurston, however, got her husband to think bigger. "Powerful men don't go running behind folks," she told him. "Folks run to see powerful men. You a mighty powerful man, John. You've paid your dues out on the road, John. It's time you reap the rewards here at home. It's time you let folks come to you, where you live."

Reverend Hurston could not quarrel with that. Once upon a time, he had been a nobody from across the creek. Now he was a respected citizen of America's first black-run incorporated town and a man of means. Mrs. Hurston had used her husband's own ego and self-image to get him right where she needed him: at home, in Eatonville.

"One moment, Mama looks drawn, pale," Zora said. "The next moment, she glows some kind of sheen. Then the sweats start. They smell, so I hope that's a sign that whatever's ailing Mama is getting outta her system."

"I can wash her bedding for you," I offered. "I'll pick it up whenever you like."

"Thank you," Zora said, and we went inside. In the kitchen, Zora's sister, Sarah, was pouring tea for my mother and hers.

"By what you're telling me," Mrs. Hurston said, glowering, "Side was probably lynched at Lake Bell. Lynched in Eatonville. In Eatonville . . ." Mrs. Hurston believed the horror, but wanted desperately to disbelieve that it had occurred in our home, our town, on our watch. "There wasn't anybody in this town to stop what happened to Terrace Side," she lamented. "My husband wasn't even here."

CHAPTER FOUR

The only way to find out how the rest of the town had weathered the assault was to go to Joe Clarke's. Though the store and porch were full of folks, only one person spoke at a time and they did so very quietly.

Bynum George said that the search party had pelted him and his wife, Maisie, with eggs from their own chickens before shooting up their coop. Dead birds littered the young couple's yard. Bertram Edges said that all the windows on his house had been smashed. A barrage of bullets had destroyed Willie Mosely's chimney, and the native South Carolinian pronounced himself lucky. The same, of course, could not be said of the fugitive, Terrace Side. He was the only known casualty of the night.

Jessie Brinks, a bowlegged peanut farmer, sat on the banister, looking like he was trying hard not to show how upset he was. "Anybody been to Lake Bell yet?" he asked.

Mr. Clarke rubbed his eyes. "Yes," he answered. "I have."

Mr. Brinks started, stopped, and started again. "What did you see?"

"Ashes, scorched earth. I'm guessing that before they burned Side, they broke him up real bad, probably pulverized that boy."

The soul of the town buckled under the weight of the murderous violence. By the front door of Joe's store, one soul in particular, the old man Chester Cools, began to show signs of collapse. Like topsoil in an earthquake, Mr. Cools started trembling and shaking, scattering from himself but staying of a piece simultaneously. Joe Clarke grabbed him under the arms, trying to support him.

"Chester, Chester! Can you hear me? Can you hear me?" Mr. Clarke barked in an effort to bring Chester back to the moment. Doc Brazzle, the town physician, took hold of Chester's chin and opened his mouth to observe the tongue. The gesture seemed to interrupt Mr. Cools's convulsions. He calmed immediately. The interest of the crowd died away almost instantly, too. Chester Cools was a fixture — a peculiar one — so was easy to dismiss. No one considered Mr. Cools dangerous or even menacing. I never did. In fact, there was only one thing about him that ever interested anyone.

The story got told that from the perch of a fine Georgia sycamore on a November night, a young Chester Cools had watched Sherman torch the Confederacy. Since little else was known about Chester Cools's past, the assumption got born that there was just little else of note about him to know.

Some men, like Joe Clarke, one of the founders of Eatonville, are legendary for their actions. Other men, like Mr. Cools, become legendary for their witness.

Mr. Cools leaned into Joe Clarke and muttered something in his ear.

Doc Brazzle had obviously overheard, judging by his pinched and puzzled expression.

When Mr. Clarke answered, it became clear what Chester Cools had said. "No. The plan to expand the town hasn't changed." Mr. Cools stared at him in silence.

Joe Clarke did what he did best: he made sense and stayed calm. "Expanding the town shouldn't worry you, Chester," Mr. Clarke said. "I better get you home. You had some sort of spell. You need rest. Everybody in this town does."

Doc Brazzle placed his hand on Mr. Cools's forehead. "A little warm," he commented. "Chester, do you have a history of——?" Dr. Brazzle paused, searching for a phrase that wouldn't insult the patient, but before he could finish, Mr. Cools came to life.

"History?" Mr. Cools asked vehemently. "Do I have a history? Well, my history is why I came here to Eatonville. I came here to escape my history. And you can be sure that's why Terrace Side came here, too. He probably thought this place could erase his history, swallow it whole, and let him start over. Instead, Terrace's history ate him alive. Just like mine. My history finished me off long ago. Because no matter how big Eatonville is or gets, history is bigger; it will finish her. It sure will."

Mr. Cools's prophecy startled everyone on the porch that day, and it caused both Doc Brazzle and Mr. Clarke to take a step back. It occurred to everyone in the town, especially Joe Clarke, that the history we were making could very well be the seed of our destruction. The raid suggested that it could be.

I had no idea when the territory of Florida officially became a part of the United States of America, but the country gained its independence from Britain in 1776. What America was for white folks in that all-important year, Eatonville became for black folks right here in America in 1887. We didn't have a White House, but we had Joe Clarke's store. Almost every man in town worked or managed his own land. Every child was enrolled in school. Sunday morning worship was better attended than the juke joint on Saturday night. Eatonville was considered a promised land for colored folk. Prosperous and industrious, Eatonville was bound to become a source of anxiety and envy for white folks sooner or later.

A month earlier, Mr. Clarke had submitted a proposal to the governor's office in Tallahassee for the expansion of Eatonville. The idea was shrewd and farsighted. Since 1887, two colored villages had formed in the square mile around our Eden. Lake Catherine came first. Then Blue Bay sprang up, and neither of the settlements was officially incorporated like Eatonville. Neither had a mayor, a marshal, nor a general store, so the people of Lake Catherine and Blue Bay naturally patronized Joe Clarke's. They frequented Eatonville's single federal building, the post office, and Mr. Calhoun had opened Eatonville's schoolhouse to their children. Since the people of Lake Catherine, Blue Bay, and Eatonville had been merging anyway, Joe Clarke suggested the union be made official with the formal redrawing of Eatonville's borders. The fledgling villages voiced hearty support for the plan, as did the folks of Eatonville. Everyone's desire was to extend the sphere of shelter. Joe Clarke intended to extend that promise to as many colored folks as he could. The fugitive Terrace Side had very likely heard of that safe harbor, that haven called Eatonville.

Mr. Clarke, his eyes shining with tears of sorrow, anger, and pride, said, "History's not a monster that devours men. It's the sum of the choices and the chances we take, if the white folks don't snatch them from us first. Our town survived last night. Our town has survived other hardships. Our town has survived for eighteen years. We'll survive the expansion, too," he continued, "and we'll be better off than we are now, stronger. When it's all done, we'll be stronger." Hope for the future invested Mr. Clarke with magnanimity. "We'll be stronger, Chester. You'll see. You don't need to be afraid. No one does."

CHAPTER FIVE

John Hurston returned to Eatonville shortly thereafter because he was presiding over services at our church, New Hope Macedonia, the following Sunday. Zora sat in the front pew with her mother, her sister, and her brother Everett, as was custom for the preacher's family. Restless as always, Zora kept looking back over her shoulder at the church's entrance. I couldn't figure out why, and my anxiousness about it might as well have sprinkled hoodoo dust on me because I *achoo*ed one hurricane of a sneeze.

"God bless you," my mother said. "And don't worry," she whispered, tapping my knee, "your time is coming."

I blinked hard. "Huh?" Then everyone in the church turned their heads. I shifted in the pew and saw sixteen-year-old Fanny Miller walking down the aisle. I turned back around and saw that a handsome stranger with a mustache like a push broom was standing at the altar next to Reverend Hurston. It was as if I had dozed off in the middle of a lesson, only waking at the critical moment.

"The reverend just announced it," my mother whispered. "Fanny's fixin' to be married."

"Married?"

"Yes." Mama squeezed my hand and dabbed at her eyes with a lilac handkerchief.

"Pairs abound in this world," Reverend Hurston began. "Soil and the ground." He gestured downward. "The clouds in the sky." He pointed up and smiled broadly as if God Himself were looking down. "There's also the pair we're celebrating this morning: the man and his wife. But God has plans for the husband and wife far beyond them staying a pair. Genesis two twenty-four reads," Reverend Hurston said, recalling from memory, "'Therefore shall a man leave his father and his mother, and shall cleave unto his wife: And they shall be one flesh.'" He paused, marking the end of the scripture, but then he pondered aloud the beauty and the aspiration in the phrase, "*One flesh*. That's what a man and his wife are: one. This ceremony is your rebirth as one new flesh." He spoke directly to the couple. "Happy birthday!"

More *Happy birthdays*, along with some *Amens*, *Sure enoughs*, and *Yes, sirs*, filled the air. During the ceremony, I thought about Teddy and how much I missed seeing him in his crisp white shirt and camel-colored suspenders on Sunday mornings. For months now he had been spending weekends at his brother Micah's place, helping to build one of the largest horse barns in Orange County. I wondered whether Teddy was sawing or hammering right then, whether the sun was hot on his shoulders, or if he was taking a break in the shade with a drink. As my mind's eye lingered on Teddy's face, Reverend Hurston boomed in conclusion, "I now pronounce you man and wife!" The words forced me to take in the couple standing before the congregation. Fanny's expression was a bit slack-jawed. The groom, whose name was Rudolph, gave a toothless smile. He looked pleased if not altogether happy.

At school, Mr. Calhoun had put Fanny in charge of checking the spelling and arithmetic of the youngest children. She managed her duties well and kept an eye on us older kids, too, often intercepting the notes passed back and forth between Hennie Clarke and Stella Brazzle. Aside from relishing the satisfaction of Fanny sabotaging Stella, I couldn't mistake my tears for amassing in a longstanding well of feeling. The slack-jawed mien that had flickered on Fanny's face after she had been pronounced somebody's wife was what petitioned my sympathy. Without embarrassing herself or her parents, Fanny had tried her best to pass a note, one written in universal code across her countenance, to the whole church. Though I had received the message loud and clear, what made me weep was that there wasn't a solitary thing for Fanny I could do.

Afterward, the congregation gathered outside on the hard clay to see the newlyweds off. Rudolph beamed so at his brown automobile, you might have thought he had just married the machine. A single small suitcase in the back seat contained all of Fanny's belongings. Next to me, Sarah was staring at the suitcase. All the while, a young man I had never seen before was staring at Sarah.

"Nice wedding," he said to Sarah with a nervous smile. "Your father is quite the preacher."

Sarah turned to the stranger, surprised. She hadn't noticed the young man standing so close. Her single onyx braid, thick and luxurious, hung over her right shoulder like a miniature stole. The young man looked as if he wanted to touch it, pet it.

"Why, yes, he is," Sarah answered somewhat hesitantly, not yet sure what to make of this tall, brown man with keen features and a pleasant voice.

He held his hand out to her. "I'm East Wheeler, a friend of Rudolph's."

"Sarah Hurston," she said, accepting East's hand. All this while, Fanny's mother was bawling. Before long, I began crying, too.

Rudolph started up the engine. Mr. and Mrs. Miller hugged and kissed Fanny goodbye one last time. Mrs. Miller held to her heart a piece of the eyelet cloth that had been used for the modest train of Fanny's wedding dress. The new bride's eyes stayed locked on her mother's. Mr. Miller grinned, relieved, I think, to be done with the expense of having a daughter and no wedding reception to pay for. The rear of Rudolph's automobile was adorned with pink ribbons and tin cans. Rudolph and Fanny waved as the new husband released the clutch, pressed the gas, and carried his bride off, spokes aglitter and the ribbons streaming.

"Had Fanny even seen that man before today?" Zora asked aloud. Reverend Hurston overheard her and put away his smiles and small talk to shoot daggers at Zora.

"If you must know," he answered, "the match had been in the making for some time. It was I who suggested the Millers move up the wedding date." John Hurston briefly paused. "After the awful, awful thing with Terrace Side, the folks in this town needed a joyous occasion. But I don't suppose a joyous marriage is something you'll ever know about, so I shouldn't be surprised at your attitude, Zora." Mr. Hurston jabbed gladly now. "Who would marry you?"

"You've got it all wrong, Daddy." Zora was not immune to her father's cruelty, but self-possession occasionally helped blunt the sting. "Who would I even want to marry? That's the real question. I can tell you one thing for sure, it won't be no preacher! Never!"

John Hurston took a step toward his daughter, but Mrs. Hurston grabbed Zora by the hand and gave her husband an affectionate and tired smile. "Just think, Zora, what a fool I must have been, falling in love with your father at first sight." Lucy Hurston's words mixed dusk and dawn. The good-humored rebuke warmed Mr. Hurston's face and calmed Zora. Then Lucy Hurston's eye caught sight of East

Wheeler sweet-talking Sarah. An internal maternal alarm instantly tensed the frail woman.

"Why, hello," Lucy Hurston said, interrupting the conversation.

East politely bowed his head. "Ma'am."

"Mama, this is East Wheeler," Sarah said a little hurriedly, embarrassed by the attention.

"Sir, it's an honor," East held out his hand to John Hurston. "I greatly enjoyed the ceremony. You delivered my friend Rudolph into matrimony in fine fashion, sir, very fine."

"Thank you," John Hurston accepted the compliment and East himself with a hearty, welcoming handshake. Zora frowned at her father and defensively planted herself at Sarah's side. Sarah shot her little sister a curious glance.

Sarah, their father's favorite, and Zora, their father's hated, had never been friends. Lucy's condition, largely playing out in their father's absence, had changed that. Viewing each other through the love of their mother, Zora and Sarah had become allies.

"Did you come very far for the wedding, Mr. Wheeler?" Lucy Hurston asked.

"No," East answered proudly. "I moved to Lake Catherine just over a month ago. I've started a coach service in these parts. Right now, I'm carrying folks in a horse and buggy, mostly to and from the train station in Maitland. Before long, I reckon, I'll have enough saved to purchase a horseless like Rudolph's."

Ambition for the material things in life further lubricated John Hurston's favorable impression of the young man. The successful striver placed an approving hand on East's athletic shoulder but played the part of minister. "It takes more than money to build something," he said. "It takes faith, too."

"I was planning on attending service again next week," East answered eagerly. He gave Sarah a quick sweet glance. "I'd like to join your flock."

Mr. Hurston said kindly, "Well, fine!"

East stepped toward Sarah, took her hand, and kissed it. "It was an honor making your acquaintance on this very special day, Miss Sarah."

Sarah nodded, blushing to the roots of her hair. "Yours, too," she managed.

Mrs. Hurston flashed the guarded grin of a white lie to East. "Don't make a stranger of yourself," she said.

The afternoon after Fanny got married, Zora and I met as we always did on Sundays at the Loving Pine. As our sacred place, it was fitting that the Loving

Pine was also Zora's study. She worked there atop a crate lid, her white paper glowing like treasure against the backdrop of the cool green forest. For as long as I could remember, Zora told stories. When she started writing them down, it seemed the most natural thing in the world.

It was a strange thing, but Zora and I never spoke about writing and she didn't talk about it.

I most hated to interrupt Zora when she stared up through the tree's canopy daydreaming. I understood innately that it was in daydreams that stories searched for spirits they considered safe harbor and, finding one, docked. Zora was one such spirit. Zora had been called to speak in this world with her pen. Her genius also required her to listen.

Zora read Rudyard Kipling's *Kim* aloud while I combed, greased, and plaited her hair. Doing something besides making lye or stirring and scrubbing laundry was sweet relief for my raw hands. Previously, we had fallen in love with the talking snake in *The Jungle Book* and had been excited to give another Kipling novel a try. We were disappointed that this one didn't have any sharp-witted animals in it, but we rooted for the Irish orphan alone in India just the same.

We were at the part in the story when Kim,

recently appointed a monk's apprentice, began learning of the Wheel of Things. One of the phenomena on the wheel, everlasting life, came at the heavy cost of dying again and again and again. I couldn't fathom the idea, not in any reasonable way, which was why it captivated and frightened me.

I made a zigzag part down the middle of Zora's head, dipped my fingers in the pomade, and oiled her scalp. I started a five-stranded braid. The woven hair reminded me of a crochet chain. Right then I wished I had some red ribbon to pull through the plaits to give them some color.

The singing drifter, Ivory, whose headless body Mr. Cools had discovered at the railroad tracks five years ago, had not entered my thoughts in a long time. Recently, however, my daydreams would turn a corner and trip over the wooden shards of his bashed guitar. Or I'd be hanging sheets and, out of the corner of my eye, think I glimpsed a tattered red ribbon like the one Ivory used as a strap. Had the horrible fate of Terrace Side conjured these fragments of my fears? Or had a benevolent force planted these warning flags?

Just then, Zora thunder-clapped the book shut. Apparently, the Wheel of Things had spun her around, too.

"Can you believe my father," she cried, "thinking that marrying off Fanny in a hurry would somehow be medicine for the town? How can it? How can a girl getting married cancel out a man getting hunted down and lynched? It doesn't make any sense."

I hesitated, then said, "I doubt one thing can really cancel out the other, but the wedding did make my mother feel better. It was a distraction."

"I'll tell you about distractions," Zora cried angrily. "With just a few looks, that East fellow practically emptied Sarah's head of everything that was in it. As for Fanny, she deserves more from her life than a husband more in love with his car than with her!

"I overheard Mr. Calhoun tell Fanny two or three times that she should apply to a teacher's college in Alabama. Now that Fanny's married, it's too late. Soon we'll hear that she's having a baby. The next time we see her, she'll have four or five children underfoot, the only pupils she'll ever have now. It's not fair!" Zora blazed.

For girls, especially colored ones like us, little was *fair*. While we never questioned our inherent value, the safety and dignity we experienced within the borders of Eatonville did not lead us to assume we should expect equality beyond them.

"I'm not getting married!" Zora declared. "Not in three years, not in three hundred years! Marriage scoops girls up and takes us out of the world. Not me. I want to travel places as far away as Lahore." Zora held up the book. "Yes, Eatonville is my home, always will be. But I don't have to hang around here and make sure Eatonville is all right. You and Teddy will do that just fine."

Her assertion floored me. "We will? How can we? Without you?"

"You'll have each other—that's how."

Until that very moment under the Loving Pine, I had never considered that there was anything about Zora that made taking up the mantle of wife or mother impossible. Zora's wheel would take her places I couldn't imagine, and provide her with experiences her books would one day testify to. I wish now I had told her that a girl like Zora Neale Hurston gets born ahead of her time so she can show folks what the future looks like. But I didn't know how to say that then. I was young and born for the calendar years that cradled my joys and suckled my sorrows.

I was lucky.

CHAPTER SIX

The world is covered in dull and sharp points alike. That's just nature's way. And there are few, if any, perfectly straight lines in nature, except maybe the horizon and the occasional thread in a spiderweb. There's a curve in every stream. Branches bend and lean. Thorns stand guard at an angle. Straight lines are man-made, and from the moment I started doing folks' laundry, I cursed men for their invention.

Before I carried my first basket of her linens down the road, Mrs. Hopson of Woodhouse Lane let me know she had fired her last girl for using too little soap and that she wouldn't pay me, "not by the pound, not on my pride," if her sheets weren't folded edge to edge, straight line on straight line, just so. I nodded, said "Yes, ma'am," and toted the basket away, wondering how that woman could look straight ahead with eyes so deeply set she resembled a flounder. Just the same, about a half dozen baskets of Mrs. Hopson's laundry later, I stood on my porch one afternoon a week before school started alongside Mama, stacking that lady's lines and boiling in my skin. Then Teddy strolled up. The sight of him blew into my front yard like an ocean breeze. He made everything flutter, especially my heart.

"What you two doing?" Teddy asked. "Nobody has any business working that hard in August."

"Well," Mama said, her voice dancing a little. "We ain't nobodies. We're somebodies. So we honor the promises we made to folks to get their things clean, August or not."

"You're the one who's hardly breaking a sweat," I said, giggling, then stepped away from my work, leaned against the porch post, and drank Teddy in.

"I do most of my chores early," Teddy said. "Pop insists. On the farm, we have to. Plus, tomorrow I'm apprenticing to Doc Brazzle."

"You being so busy reminds me," Mama said, "think you and Micah can make time soon to come by and remove the well cap? We're running out faster than usual with all the washing we're doing."

Teddy nodded, as though adding the chore to his mental list. "You two women don't have no business with that heavy limestone cover. On a day like this one, the only business anyone should have is with a swim hole. It's too hot for anything else. Let's go swimming," Teddy said.

"Look around here." I gestured. "Do we look finished?"

"You will be if I help," Teddy said, stepping up on the porch and lifting a sheet from the ironing board. I grabbed the other end and the cotton stretched between us like the blank slate of a shared future. Alone, the orderliness and predictability of work often numbed me. With Mama and Teddy, I might as well have been dancing around a maypole. Feigning ignorance and looking away, I brushed my cheek with Teddy's when we matched corners. Each time the sheet became a more perfect, smaller square, Teddy gave my ear a quick nuzzle perfectly timed to avoid my mother's glance. It didn't hurt that Mrs. Baker had done just as good a job teaching her boys how to do housework as my Mama had me. In a delighted flash, we were finished.

"Where shall it be," Teddy asked, "Blue Sink?"

"Yep," I said, pulling off my scarf and untucking the braid at the nape of my neck. For Mama, it was undoing her apron and hanging it on the back of the white folks' pantry door that signaled the official end of her workday. For me, it was taking off my scarf.

"I like your single braid," Teddy said. "You look womanish."

"Flattery won't get you more than my hand," I said, holding it out to him. Mama frowned playfully at the thought of him having that much.

"That's enough," Teddy said, and kissed my wrist.

Mama smiled, pleased with how lightheartedly and tenderly Teddy treated me.

"Have fun, now," she said.

We did. We walked closely together through the coppice of runty cedars on the sandbank beyond my house, smiling and laughing at nothing at all. The sandbank overlooked a clearing of pale-pink bearberry. Teddy picked a few blossoms and set them in my hair. Then he knelt; I got on his back and he carried me, as if I weighed little more than his clothes, across the clearing, through the cool woods, and nearly to Blue Sink's bank.

We spied Zora swinging her feet over the edge.

Teddy let me down and called after her: "What you doing sitting instead of swimming?"

Zora stood, hand on hip; she turned to face us. "I've been waiting on you two."

Teddy stripped down to a light pair of knickers, his clothes a denim puddle at his feet. While Teddy politely focused on how the wind parted the rows of Spanish moss draped on the old willow, Zora and I quickly stripped down to bloomers and chemises. I felt prickly and pointed in a body that had rounded out and softened. I swallowed hard. Zora counted, "One, two, three!"

We jumped. We swam. We climbed up the mossy rocks and stepped to the edge, where we jumped and swam again and again. Finally, exhausted, we returned to our clothes and walked off from Blue Sink just like that, the way we always did, like it was nothing at all. If we had known that was the last time ever that the three of us would swim there together, we might have lingered long into the evening. Thunder and lightning would have had trouble driving us away. But endings in life don't often do us the courtesy of declaring themselves, the way they do in books with the last words on the last page.

Stories are similar to man-made straight lines. Life is not.

CHAPTER SEVEN

The next day, Zora helped me haul laundry, and on our way home, we stopped by Mr. Cools's place near the border with Maitland. Mr. Cools had a turnip patch, a half-blind mule named Girly, and the best peaches for three counties. He didn't mind folks coming onto his property for the occasional peach, and that's what Zora and I were in the mood for. His strangeness aside, Mr. Cools nevertheless deserved — and got — folks' respect and restraint.

Girly stood snorting in her split-rail yard, so we knew Mr. Cools was home. We knocked on his cabin door to ask his permission to pick a few peaches. "Mr. Cools," Zora called. "Mr. Cools."

A minute passed without an answer, so we figured he was napping or something. Girly snorted and whipped her tail, egging us on. So we gathered up peaches in the skirts of our dresses and fed the mule as many as she could eat. Satisfied, she trotted away to the other side of the yard. Dismissed by Girly, we gathered a few peaches for ourselves, then sat under the tree to eat them. I don't know how much time had passed — maybe ten minutes, maybe an hour — when we heard a loud thud come from Mr. Cools's house. That was followed by whining, like the sound a small child might make after a spill.

I tried not to worry. "Something must have just fallen over in there or was dropped."

"What if it was Mr. Cools? What if he fell down?" We got up and walked over to the cabin and peered into a window. "Mr. Cools," Zora spoke at the glass. "You all right in there?"

In place of a curtain, a brown sack too short and too narrow to cover the entire pane hung there. Around the edges of the sack covering, I could see into the room. A table, a trunk, and a threadbare chair were all piled against the front door. Suddenly Zora

jumped, startled, and the back of her head crashed
into my face. The surprise, more than the collision,
knocked me to the ground. I looked up. The old sack
had been pushed aside.

On the Florida frontier, we lived with gators, bob-
cats, and cottonmouths in our midst. Danger lurked,
snorted, snapped, and was hungry all around us con-
stantly. Mr. Cools stood there in the window, one of
the world's deadliest sights: a frightened man aiming a
gun. The gun, pointed squarely at us, was worse than
any wild animal. I couldn't help but recall the terror I
felt when those white men burst into my home with
their dogs.

Zora kept her head. "It's us," she said, pointing
to herself and then to me, "Zora and Carrie." Chester
Cools tapped the glass with the rifle barrel as if making sure the window was still between him and us. The
action startled me to my feet, but we were still very
much in range of a bullet. I think it was our fear that
finally made us recognizable to him. The wild shine of
his eyes dulled, and the panic left him. Without it, he
began to cave in and unravel.

"Go away!" he howled piteously. "I ain't bin here,
or anywhere, for a long, long time!"

Tears mingled with the sweat on Mr. Cools's

collapsed face. Zora pressed her palm to the window. It was as close as she could get to touching his cheek, to comforting him. "We're not going anywhere," she cooed. "In fact, we'll stay here as long as you need us," she promised, placing urgency and kindness one on top of the other. "Come out here with us, Mr. Cools, and together we'll go tell Mr. Clarke that something's bothering you. Just put down the gun. Please!"

Mr. Cools shook his head, like a shriveled blossom dangling from a broken stem. "I ain't bin Chester Cools for a long time," he said sadly. A vein bulged in his forehead. "I bin dead!" Now he was shouting. "DEAD, I SAY!"

My skin crawled and my scalp tingled. As much as his shocking words were nonsense, for a moment, they made sense; they matched his shattered, grotesque face. Zora shuddered and I pulled at her arm to leave. But her curiosity and compassion kicked in.

"No, you're not," Zora said. "How could that be? How?"

But reason would not change Chester's mind. "I'm dead! Now, go on, git! You run from this zombie if you know what's good for you!" Chester Cools waved the rifle barrel around so wildly it resembled a snake. The weapon discharged. We screamed. Wood pulp exploded from the roof. Zora and I grabbed hands and our feet motored, headed for the place we'd always gone in an emergency: Joe Clarke's.

Willie Mosely was dozing in a rocker on Joe's porch when we came stampeding up the steps and startled him awake.

"What you gals doing, waking me up all hurly-burly like that? Mighty rude," Mr. Mosely charged.

In its burlap sling, Willie Mosely's broken arm looked like a small sack of vegetables tied to his chest. Bo Wilson, a struggling sharecropper, appeared behind the screen door. "Hold your horses," he said, then stepped out on the porch. One look at us and his narrow face became serious. "What's this about?"

"Chester Cools," Zora blurted out, "he needs help! He's saying—" She stopped. "Strange *things*. He lost control and fired his gun!"

News of the gun going off alarmed both men. "Anybody hurt?" Willie Mosely asked.

"We don't know!" I said desperately. "Maybe Mr. Cools is, him acting so strange!"

"Slow down and tell us what happened," Mr. Wilson said.

"Mr. Cools has barricaded himself in his house!" Zora replied.

"A barricade?" Confusion marked Mr. Wilson's face. "To protect himself from what?"

"We don't know!" Zora insisted, impatient. She did not say anything about a zombie. "Where is Mr. Clarke? We need Mr. Clarke!"

"Joe's in Tallahassee today, seeing about the expansion," Mr. Wilson said. "I'm minding the store. Willie, would you watch the store while I go get Doc Brazzle? He needs to pay Chester a visit."

"What can Brazzle do 'bout a man shooting off a gun in his own house?" Willie asked. "Other than get shot himself?"

"Chester's not going to shoot anybody. And if Chester's hurt himself, Doc can help. If Chester hasn't hurt himself, maybe Doc can talk some sense into him. Are you going to watch the store or aren't you?"

"Sure I will. But I don't like how none of this sounds."

"Neither do I," Mr. Wilson agreed. "But somebody's gotta alert Brazzle if Chester is sick or crazy."

"Or both," Willie declared. Mr. Wilson left for Doc Brazzle's.

"Don't get shot," Willie called after him. When Mr. Wilson was out of view, Willie turned and gave us a hard stare.

"Sorry we woke you," Zora said. "How's your arm?"

"On holiday," Willie said. "Unfortunately, it's put the rest of me out of work, too." Looking at me, Willie continued, "Teddy was with Doc Brazzle when he set my arm. If Teddy were a little older, a little stronger, I would have let him set the bone."

"I'll tell him," I said, smiling with pride. Teddy was famous in Eatonville for the animal hospital he had built outside one of his family's barns. An assortment of pens and cages housed wild and domesticated animals alike. The men who came to the Baker farm to buy seed from Mr. Baker began picking Teddy's brain on the health of their livestock. Doc Brazzle caught wind of the boy's expertise and thought Teddy could easily learn to treat humans. Doc Brazzle asked Mr. Baker if Teddy could serve as his apprentice. Mr. Baker liked the idea. People can tell you what hurts and don't generally peck, bite, or scratch. Teddy agreed.

"In fact, don't tell the doc this," said Willie, "but I think Teddy might have a better chance of getting through to Chester than he does."

"Why do you say that?" Zora asked.

"Teddy knows animals," he said, "and that's just

what Chester is sounding like right now — a scared animal."

As we learned later, Bo Wilson arrived at Doc Brazzle's only to find the doctor away in Orlando for the day. So Mr. Wilson left a message with his daughter, Stella, before hurrying on to Mr. Cools's farm. He arrived around four, spied the makeshift barricade through the window, and something more: Chester sound asleep in his bed. Bo Wilson took that as an improvement upon the situation. Sleep, he decided, had stepped in to do Chester a favor and prevent an accident from occurring with the gun. Relieved, Bo Wilson went back to the store and closed at the customary time, six o'clock.

Mr. Clarke returned to Eatonville around midnight. The first he had heard of any trouble with Chester was the following morning when Mr. Wilson went by the porch to hear how things had gone in Tallahassee.

Nearly twenty-four hours after Zora had tried to persuade Mr. Cools that Mr. Clarke could help him, Mr. Clarke finally arrived on the small farm with Doc Brazzle in tow. Smashing down the door after knocking got them no answer, the two men found Mr.

Cools where Bo Wilson had last seen him, in bed. No blood. No gunshot wound. Just Chester Cools: stiff, dead, gone. Doc Brazzle examined the body. Chester Cools had died of a heart attack.

Mr. Clarke had known Chester longer than anyone else in town had, and to the best of his knowledge, Chester Cools had no family, so Mr. Clarke handled the funeral arrangements. He asked Doc Brazzle to prepare the body for burial, and Teddy assisted. Mr. Clarke asked Bertram Edges to smith silver funerary spikes for the coffin. The blacksmith dutifully carried out the request. And Mr. Clarke asked John Hurston, who rarely did carpentry work anymore, to build the box and officiate at the service. John Hurston did both.

John Hurston and Joe Clarke were men linked by historical circumstance, men who chose to live in the same place for the same reasons: a conviction that black people have the right to live freely and to own their own things. Other than that, there was no personal tie. They were friendly but not friends. They didn't share a bottle of spirits an evening or two a week like Mr. Clarke and Mr. Edges did, or hunt together, or visit each other, ever.

Mr. Cools had not been a churchgoing man. John

Hurston respected that. He led the Lord's Prayer at the grave, nothing more. Except for Lucy Hurston, who wasn't feeling up to it, the whole town attended, as was custom with every funeral of an Eatonville resident. The solemn mood, though, never gave way to grief, tears. Standing between Teddy and Zora at the cemetery, I couldn't help but chide myself for feeling so much sadder after Fanny's wedding than I did at Mr. Cools's funeral.

CHAPTER EIGHT

A few days after the funeral, Zora, Teddy, and I met at the Loving Pine and wandered south from there, where we discovered that a morning downpour must have swamped up the fields. Mosquitoes and no-see-ums whirred and buzzed above the murky puddles of standing water. I hardly looked up I was so busy swatting and slapping the bloodsuckers and mud flecks on my ankles and shins.

"Tonight, we gonna need pounds of baking soda paste for these bites!" Teddy prescribed. "This is as bad as it's been all summer!"

"It's worse than it's been all summer," I corrected.

"At the end of summer, it's always bad," Zora said. Then, as if considering what else the season held, she reminded us: "When we start school in a week, we'll be the oldest kids. The oldest! Can you believe it?"

"We're not one hundred, Zora. We're fourteen," Teddy shot back. "We're not dying! We're growing up!"

Along with Stella Brazzle and a few others, we were poised to take our place as Mr. Calhoun's most advanced pupils. Our school only went up to eighth grade. The high schools for coloreds were in cities. The nearest one to Eatonville was a boarding school in Jacksonville. No one we knew had gone. Zora's brother Bob worked as a field hand for three years before he attended pharmacy school. After eighth grade, the Baker boys worked their family farm before starting homesteads of their own. I knew that Teddy would not follow in their footsteps. The likelier path for him was the kind Doc Brazzle had carved by attending the Meharry Medical College in Tennessee, one of the first and only black medical schools in the country.

The shape of Zora's future was as hazy as Teddy's was sharply focused. Mr. and Mrs. Hurston would probably allow Zora to continue her studies with Mr. Calhoun beyond eighth grade, but I doubted Lucy Hurston would let Zora go live alone in Jacksonville to attend high school. There was no doubt she wanted more education for her bright, shining girl, but she didn't seem ready to let the world be her baby's teacher.

"I'm aware of how old we are," Zora said, scoffing. "What you're not acknowledging or aware of is that growing up means something different for me and Carrie than it does for you."

"What do you mean?" Teddy was genuinely confused.

"However much I'd like to read and study the world over under tree canopies and great minds alike, I just can't see yet how that's going to happen, not yet anyway, with Mama sick and my father holding all the purse strings." Zora acknowledged her challenge but didn't fully concede to defeat.

"Lord, Zora!" Teddy said. "You're the smartest person at school. Not the smartest *girl*. The smartest *person*, period! You could go to high school. You could go to college, for grief's sake! I know you could and so does everybody else in this town!"

Teddy was right. Everyone did know that Zora

was capable of tackling those things. But it was up to Zora alone to figure out how to make them happen. As we got older, the way to that path would only grow tougher. What constituted a person — being mean or sweet spirited, vindictive or kind, jealous or generous — mattered little or not at all against the weight of facts out of our control. Life was decided by men being men, women being women, some folks being white, others being black, and too many souls finding themselves piss-poor instead of well fed for no good reason.

"As a man, even a colored one," Zora told Teddy, "the world, here and there, could be your oyster. On the other hand, where Carrie and I are concerned, the world has been well primed to hand us lists of places we could prepare oysters, serve them, and clean up the shells." Zora turned and spoke directly to me: "I hate to think of anyone, especially you, spending years—" She sighed deeply.

"Taking care of white folks, like my mama," I finished.

"Yes."

"There's no shame in tending folks," I said. "Least of all folks like you two!" I took Zora's hand, she grabbed Teddy's, and the three of us formed a chain.

It wasn't a chain made of silver, platinum, or gold. It was forged of a stronger mettle, mined from lifelong friendship composed of love.

Our embrace loosened and we regained our bearings. Surprisingly, not heading anywhere in particular, we were closer to the Grounds, Eatonville's cemetery, than anything else. June through October, just a flutter beyond the boneyard, layers of vines smothered the trees and sculpted them into a sweet pig face. November through May, the foliage thinned out and the sweet pig face was replaced by a wolf snout. Though it was only August, the face leering at us was more lupine than porcine.

"Oh, Lord. Look!" Zora yelled, pointing toward the graveyard. "Oh," she yelled again, and bolted. Teddy and I tore off after, running down a short slope, through the cemetery gate and between uneven slate markers. We caught up to her at the edge of a six-foot-deep gash in the ground.

Planted in the dirt like an upright floorboard, the coffin lid looked thin and flimsy. The coffin contained only a few clumps of earth. Otherwise it was empty.

Chester Cools had been stolen from his grave.

Zora was dumbstruck. Teddy doubled over and

heaved. My skin crawled with gooseflesh. Disbelief threatened to swallow us whole. *Maybe all nightmares are really one single, continuous nightmare,* I thought. And the nightmare was about one thing: emptiness.

A black automobile came sailing down the road and stopped at the cemetery gate. It was Mr. Ambrose driving his horseless. Mr. Clarke rode beside him.

"Snidlets," Mr. Ambrose called, using his nickname for Zora, which he had given her on the day she was born.

One January morning, the way Mr. Ambrose told it, he was chopping pork on a table John Hurston had built when the wealthy old-timer recollected the carpenter was up in Jacksonville on a job while Lucy remained at home heavy with child. Mr. Ambrose went by the house to see how Lucy was doing and discovered the exhausted and elated woman cradling a mint-new baby girl. Fate had assigned Jude Ambrose the honor of cutting Zora's belly cord. From that day forward, he called her Snidlets.

"Mr. Cools's grave!" Zora cried.

"Yes, I know," Mr. Ambrose said simply, sadly, climbing out of his car.

Mr. Clarke got out of the car, too, then pulled a handkerchief from his pocket. He removed his hat and wiped the sweat from his brow. His expression was jagged and grim. "Why are y'all here?" he asked.

"We were just wandering," Teddy answered flatly. When I think back on it now, Teddy had already started looking pale then.

"The thought settled on me to pay my respects to Chester this afternoon, and I ain't got the slightest idea why," Mr. Ambrose explained. "Other than some things play angel whistles and some other things blow demon whistles."

"Which whistle you suppose called you out here?" Zora asked. "The angel one or the demon one?"

Some men are above being questioned by women and children, let alone a colored girl child. Mr. Ambrose had too much respect for intelligence to be such a man.

"Whichever call it was, I imagine it's the same one that you heard, too."

"Jude, why don't you carry these kids home," Mr. Clarke ordered gently. "I'm going to look around here a bit."

"I'll drive them on and come back for you," Mr. Ambrose answered.

"Don't bother. After you drop the kids, would you go by Bertram Edges's place and tell him to bring my horse out here? That will do me just fine."

Zora erupted. "Mr. Clarke, you can't stay here alone!"

"The gang of resurrection men already took what they came for: the body," Mr. Clarke said, sounding exhausted, even defeated. "The only other things of value here were the silver coffin nails." He paused to look at the coffin. "The resurrection men got those, too. They not coming back."

I had only heard the term *resurrection men* a few times, but I knew it meant grave robbers. On starless nights, resurrection men gripped shovels, clenched lanterns, and disturbed the dead to steal valuables or to purloin corpses and sell them to scientists and medical schools. Mr. Cools had died once. It felt like the resurrection men had killed him again.

"It's surprising that something like this hasn't happened before, with the laws on the books outlawing medical schools from using white folks as cadavers," Mr. Clarke said. "Chances are Chester's body is on ice in a train car by now, headed for a fancy medical school up north. There's nothing I can do about it. At this point, no one can."

Teddy winced, seeming genuinely confused as he parsed out the absurd paradox of ranking people on the basis of skin color, even after they were dead. "Doctors cut into our bodies, our black bodies, because they don't consider us people," he said. "But then we come to define in their books and manuals," Teddy finished, "what's human."

"That day Mr. Cools threatened Carrie and me"—Zora stopped—"Mr. Cools told us something, something about not being human, that makes sense to me now. I don't think his grave was robbed."

"What are you talking about?" Mr. Clarke said slowly in a low voice, the muscles in his jaw working.

"That he was a zombie! We should have said something on that day," Zora professed. "But you weren't at the store, and then I figured it was just another crazy Chester thing. But now it doesn't seem so crazy anymore, his empty grave and all."

"Tell us, Zora," Mr. Ambrose said gently, patiently. "What did Chester Cools say to you and Carrie?"

"That he was—and has been for a long time—not himself. That he was a zombie."

For a full ten seconds, there was stricken silence. Then, "You're speaking ill of the dead," Mr. Clarke charged, his voice hard. "Chester Cools was no monster, Zora. He was a man, plain and simple."

"The desecration of this grave is what is monstrous here," Mr. Ambrose broke in. "Zora, we owe Chester Cools our respect; he deserves dignity."

"If folks heard that Chester said he was a zombie," Mr. Clarke said, exasperated, "no matter how ridiculous that is or how crazy Chester was, some people could use that against us. I wouldn't put it past white folks to accuse Eatonville of black magic. I wouldn't put it past them to burn the place down in the name of religion or safety or some other madness."

Zora, for the time, accepted Joe Clarke's admonition, but she also challenged him to execute justice. "So, are you going to go after the men who took Chester?" she asked. "If you recover Mr. Cools's body and put it back in the ground, where it belongs, folks will know exactly what happened and everyone can rest in peace."

"Oh, Zora," Mr. Clarke said, disappointment in his voice. "You know very well that a colored law man can't pursue white men or expect justice from them. Besides, while desecration is an abomination, it's not murder. What matters is that Chester departed this world in his own time.

"So you three promise me something?" Mr. Clarke asked.

I looked at Zora while Teddy and Zora looked at Mr. Clarke.

"Promise you what?" Zora asked.

"Promise you will not mention Chester's talk about zombies to anyone."

Like Mr. Clarke, I believed that in the grips of some fit or fever dream, Chester Cools had told us a strange lie that, to him, was truth. Unlike Mr. Clarke, however, I still believed in magic, too. Maybe the most magical thing in life is how extraordinarily awful things, like grave robberies and lynchings, can exist alongside ordinary things like working, shopping, or just walking and talking. Maybe the true magic in this life is that even after facing and experiencing horror, we can still carry on with the ordinary. That's what Mr. Clarke was asking us to do: to help prop up ordinary life, itself a magical and wondrous thing, with silence and a secret.

"Yes," I pledged.

"Me too," Teddy said.

"Zora?" Mr. Clarke needed to hear from her. She covered her face with her hands so she could think. When she finished thinking, she looked up, the color drained from her face. She looked sick to her stomach.

"Zora?" Mr. Clarke entreated.

I suspect she found the federation of a secret more palatable than the exile of a tattler. "Yes," she answered.

Mr. Ambrose placed his hand on Zora's arm. "Come on, now. I'm taking y'all home."

CHAPTER NINE

Most people in town believed that, in all likelihood, resurrection men had taken Chester's body, motivated by nothing more than greed. Still, a few other theories circulated.

Some folks whispered that Joe Clarke's ambition to expand an all-colored town had inspired devilish white men to chase a fugitive across our border, then capture and kill him as a warning to us and others. First, that we were too ambitious. Second, that not even Eatonville was completely safe from the white man's cruel power. Their greatest hope, perhaps, was that we would pack up our experiment of self-government.

Nature wasn't being too welcoming Herself. A mini-drought had taken hold between Lake Catherine and Blue Sink. The goldenrod and Queen Anne's lace shriveled. The palmettos at the bases of the trees had shrunk and grown jaundiced, exposing nests of snake eggs to owls and the frying sun. Withered and matted, the Bermuda grass smelled of kindling. At the same time, over in Blue Bay, hard rains had driven up the water in the lake and several families had been flooded out. Clouds of mosquitoes and gnats hovered over them like clouds of fine mesh. The simultaneity of the extremes was more than unsettling.

Three days to the hour after the discovery of Chester Cools's empty grave, Zora and I were walking to Blue Sink, still trying to make sense of it all.

"For years in school, from our readers," she said, "we've learned about Greek gods, Roman gods, and Norse gods. And in church, we get an earful 'bout the Christian God. About how Jesus Christ died on the cross, then rose again. That basically boils down to one thing," Zora said. "Jesus Christ was a zombie."

At first, I bristled at the way she dared to challenge orthodoxy. But then my affection for Zora and my confidence in our intellects tempered my outrage. I didn't have to agree, but I could certainly listen.

"Yet folks will never come out and call Christ a zombie. Why? Because zombie stuff is voodoo stuff and voodoo stuff is not Christian stuff. But both are supernatural stuff," she continued. "Mr. Clarke thinks the grave robbery is about plain old natural folks — black folks and white folks here on Earth — nothing else. I respect Mr. Clarke, but I think what happened to Chester is about something else and other worlds."

"Oh, I wouldn't go as far to Heaven or Hades with it," Old Lady Bronson intoned, startling both Zora and me out of our respective skins, which I'm sure tickled the age-old power. Her trusted fishing pole at her side, she stepped out of the westerly palm grove.

Old Lady Bronson wore a long brown shift dress with two large pockets. Her long, silver braid was pinned into a spiral at the nape of her neck. When I was very young, I feared the ancient woman. When I learned that she had been young once, and a new-comer to America itself, my fear became fascination. My fascination morphed into respect and admiration.

Zora's eyes were aflame and her skin red, flushed.

Zora gave the midwife and healer a hug. "How long have you been back?" she asked.

Old Lady Bronson sighed. "Long enough." Old Lady Bronson wasn't the kind of woman who had to be told things to have knowledge of them. What could we tell her that she didn't already know, about Chester, about anything?

All of Old Lady Bronson's children lived up north. For the better part of the summer, Old Lady Bronson had been visiting her granddaughter Billie in Cape May, New Jersey. Billie and her husband owned and ran a boardinghouse and had two young children besides. So Old Lady Bronson had traveled north to lend a hand until school started back up.

"While you were in New Jersey, did you go to New York City?" Zora asked. "Did you?" She was about ready to pop.

"No." Old Lady Bronson laughed, knowing Zora wouldn't forgive her for missing such an opportunity. "What interest you have in anything *new*, anyways? By the sound of it, you more taken with the old places and ways. . . ."

"By the sound of what?" Zora asked.

Old Lady Bronson crowed. "You talking with Carrie about gods like you know a few. I'll tell you one thing. This ain't how folks talk up in Jersey. I'm glad to be home in the company of your awfully fine mind, Zora. Glad to be home."

"We're awfully glad you're home, too," I said, with so much feeling that I surprised myself a little.

"Now, about that conversation you were having: God is pure spirit. Jesus is spirit made flesh. People are flesh blessed with spirit. Zombies are cursed flesh with no spirit at all." Old Lady Bronson informed us matter-of-factly. "Heaven ain't on their itinerary."

The spiraled braid at the base of Old Lady Bronson's neck came loose and uncoiled like a gray serpent stretching its spine.

"In my village, when I was a mere girl—younger than the two of you," Old Lady Bronson began, "the fate of the living dead was thought to have befallen a bride-to-be called Novelette. I have never heard another story like it. It's not a story I've ever told before or will ever tell again."

We sat with bated breath. Time travelers are real and everywhere. The most experienced ones are called old people. A hostage of history as a young woman, the length of Old Lady Bronson's years had transformed her into a caretaker of the past.

Old Lady Bronson continued: "Novelette was

engaged to a merchant from Port-au-Prince. Three days before the ceremony, the wedding party journeyed to a mountain spring for a picnic celebration. A mixed-blood named Jacques Callier owned the coffee plantation on which the spring was situated and attended the gathering. The village below listened to the revelers sing for hours to the drumbeat of happiness. It was a beautiful song of anticipation and light. That light was quickly extinguished. The party over, Novelette, her fiancé, and the entire wedding party set out on their return to our village, but just steps from the village well, Novelette fell ill. The next afternoon, on what would have been the eve of her wedding day, she died. On the morning she was to sail to France with her merchant from Port-au-Prince as a wife, the young beauty was buried.

"Months later, while Novelette's family and fiancé were still mourning, a well digger in our village, Jean, received a letter from Jacques Callier. Callier was requesting the well digger's help in devising a new irrigation plan for his crops. The mountain spring Callier's plantation relied upon had dried up. This was the same spring where Novelette's wedding party had enjoyed their picnic.

"Jean the well digger set out one morning for

what we all thought would be a month away of work. By supper of the same day, Jean returned to the village. Shaking with terror, he claimed to have seen Novelette on Callier's plantation. But the Novelette he saw, he told us, smelled like rotten meat and her eyes had been sewn shut. Jean recognized that it was Novelette because she had a pink wing-shaped birthmark near her ear. Jean begged her to speak to him. She could only make droning, clicking sounds. Jean saw others there with their eyes sewn shut—men, women, and children. Some had grown scales, like armor, where burns had healed and scarred. None could speak—could only make those noises, like a machine.

"Jean's tale drove Novelette's fiancé wild with grief. The merchant ran to Novelette's resting place and dug up his beloved's grave. He unearthed an empty coffin. In a fury, he traveled to Callier's plantation to demand Novelette's release. Where the Callier manor once stood, he found only cinders, ashes."

The gleam of a good yarn that had lit Old Lady Bronson's face began to fade. "For years afterward," she said, "stories spread of the ghost of a burned Jacques Callier haunting the countryside, crying only one word: Novelette, Novelette, Novelette."

Old Lady Bronson closed the door on the world of her childhood and reentered the world of ours. The peek into her history granted Zora some new tools with which she might interpret our last encounter with Chester Cools.

"Could Chester have spent his life here in Eatonville hiding from someone like this Callier?" Zora asked. "Mr. Cools barricaded himself in his house like he was trying to keep something or someone out."

"Oh, Zora." Old Lady Bronson's rich alto tried to soothe. "Chester wasn't hiding," she said. "He was sick, not stalked. He was hindered by the harness of his own mind."

Zora frowned deeply. She trusted Old Lady Bronson, but she also heeded her gut. "Are you sure?" Zora challenged. "He drew a gun on us. Why would he have done that if he hadn't been trying to protect himself? Why?"

"Maybe he was scared," Old Lady Bronson answered, "of what demons his own mind conjured." Zora didn't look like she was buying it. Old Lady Bronson smiled wisely. "Or maybe he was simply scared of dying. It's not unheard of, you know."

CHAPTER TEN

The next morning, I threaded my single braid with white ribbon on the porch swing. For Teddy's delight and my pride, I gingerly touched my hair to make sure every strand was smooth. Surely Teddy would pick me up for the first day of school. Last year we had gotten in the habit of quizzing each other on our walks in preparation for geometry and geography exams. Other times, mostly when we held hands, we were silent. For this upcoming school year, my fingers were crossed that we had matured enough to hold hands and talk at the same time.

From the perch of the porch swing, I watched a dark silhouette come sauntering down the sand dune, in between the cedars. The figure reached out to touch the bark, as if for luck, in a familiar gesture. I leaped from the swing. *My Teddy's early!* I thought. As the figure grew nearer, my excitement turned to horror.

The thing was, but it wasn't. The curling edges of a gaping black splotch marked the boundary between bottomless nothing and everything else. Fear nailed my feet to the porch floor. I tried to cry out, but only swirls of smoke floated from my mouth. The darkness before me swallowed the smoke, then spat it back at me in the form of pure sound. I can only describe it as a medley of loss. Ivory gently strumming his guitar; the tap of Mr. Cools's rifle on the windowpane; my father's cheery whistle floating, untethered, in the shadowy distance. Then thunderous gongs exploded in my ear, a bell tolling just for me.

I woke in a cold sweat, panting and clutching at my ears. Mama sat beside me, holding a large stirring spoon, a metal pot in her lap.

"Thank goodness something finally woke you!" She set down the pot and spoon and hugged me. "You've been murmuring and shaking, Carrie. I couldn't wake you! Her embrace tightened. "You're safe now. You're safe!"

"I had a bad dream, Mama, a really bad dream."

"Oh, baby." She rocked me. "It's over . . . all over. Maybe you should stay home today. What do you think? I'll stay home with you."

"It's the first day of school, Mama. I have to go. I wanna go." More than anything I wanted to get out of bed, throw off the nightmare, and get dressed.

Mama pushed some of my sweat-dampened hair behind my ears. "I know that. What I'm wondering is if you're up to it."

I sat taller on my cot. "I'm fine."

"You'll need a good breakfast," she said, relenting with a sorrowful half smile.

"Thank you."

"You just take it easy, you hear?"

"I will."

Mama left the room. I breathed deeply in an effort to steel myself. The first day of the last year of school I'd complete with Zora and Teddy was here, today. And I had to be ready for it. I changed out of my nightclothes into a camisole and slip. I brushed my hair and then gave myself one braid, run through with pale-pink ribbon. Nearly ready when Teddy arrived, I listened to his exchange with Mama from the bedroom as I put on my shift dress. The familiarity between my mother and my beau had a funny affect. Occasionally, the only way the two could be completely comfortable with each was to act overly formal. That always amused me.

"Good morning, Mrs. Brown." I could hear the nervous smile in his voice. "Those eggs I hear frying in the skillet?" he asked.

"Expecting we would have a guest this morning, I made extra. Come right in. Have a seat."

"I'll wait for Carrie, thank you, ma'am."

I came out of my room, and unable to call the hour unequivocally good on account of my nightmare, I settled on a plain "Morning." Teddy gave me a shy and tentative little smile.

Teddy pulled out my chair. I sat, recognizing how much more I preferred doing things with Teddy than him doing things for me. Mama placed three plates on the table and then an egg on each of those. Mama sat down, still wearing her apron, blessed the meal, then gave us permission to "dig in." I picked up the small serving platter and passed the hot-water corn bread to Teddy.

"Teddy," Mama asked, "how is your mother doing, with both of your brothers married off now and gone?"

"Mama said she always wished for daughters, ma'am. Now she has some, in my brothers' wives. She loves them."

"And how's your apprenticeship with Doc Brazzle?" Mama asked him.

"It's good. Doc Brazzle is an attentive physician, and it's easy to learn from him. I daresay, though, that we both have something to learn from you."

"What about?" Mama asked incredulously.

"About sewing, ma'am. I watched Doc Brazzle needle Maisie George's forehead shut a day ago. The entire time, I was thinking it was too bad for Maisie that he couldn't make stitches as neat and tidy as I know yours to be."

"Hems and collars sewn on cotton are quite different from making stitches in skin," she said. "What happened to Maisie?"

"She told us she tripped weeding the fields on the Pearson place and sliced her head open on a hoe."

"We all know Bynum went upside her head," I said quietly, angry.

Teddy didn't agree or disagree. "Doc Brazzle

thinks Bynum discouraged her from leaving the field sooner for the sake of her day's pay."

Mama shook her head in disbelief.

Teddy swallowed, then said, "Micah told my parents that right after he and Daisy got married, Daisy asked him when he was going to start beating her."

Mama's eyes got wide. My stomach nearly leaped off a roof. "What? Does Micah plan on hitting Daisy?"

"No, of course not," Teddy answered.

"Then why in the world would she ask that?" I was beside myself.

"Daisy's folks still work the land in Sanford where her grandma and her daddy were born slaves."

"So?" I answered.

"My mama thinks the folks that stay on the land where they were slaves treat each other bad because that's all they've known. Daisy hails from people who ain't risen out of all there was to slavery yet, like the beating and humiliating and driving people down. Daisy's daddy beats up on her mama, her mama hits him back, and all her brothers and sisters are fighting and hopping mad all the time, stomping from their cabin to the fields and back. 'Cause that's the only life Daisy's known, she was asking my brother if that's the only kinda life she's *ever* gonna know."

"Didn't Daisy ever go to school somewhere?" I asked.

"Nope. I'll be the first of my brothers to marry an educated woman."

Mama glowed. I backed away from the table. "We better get going," I said.

Mama stood and accompanied us to the porch. I kissed her cheek. "Bye, Mama."

"Wait a second." Mama pointed to the stand of cedars near our house. "Somebody's coming."

A tall figure was walking casually down the hill in our direction. I spied a bowler hat, and some kind of metal, probably a belt buckle, glinted in the light.

"I think it's that fellow who took a shine to Sarah Hurston," Mama said. "Remember, Carrie? We met him after Fanny's wedding."

"Oh," I answered flatly. "East Wheeler."

"Yes, that's him." Mama waved the handsome figure on. East Wheeler picked up his pace.

When he arrived in our dooryard, East Wheeler removed his brown bowler. "Good morning," he said cheerfully.

"Good morning," Mama responded, friendly but curious. Teddy shook East's hand and introduced himself.

"It's nice to see you, Mr. Wheeler," Mama said. "What brings you here this morning?"

"Well," East said, getting into it quicker than many might have, rightly assessing forthrightness to be a better tack than flavorless small talk: "I was doing a passenger pickup in Maitland the day before yesterday, and I overheard some women talking about the fine laundress your Carrie is and how it's a shame that one girl hauls so many loads by herself."

Teddy crimsoned at the mention of my doing so much hard work alone. For some reason, his shame bothered me. "Yes. What of it?" I prompted.

"I got to thinking," he continued. "Maybe I can be of help and deliver some of those loads for you with my coach."

Mama had nothing against East, but she wasn't anybody's fool, either. "For how much?"

East pretended to consider what I believe he had already decided. "A nickel for every half mile from pickup to drop-off." He held his hat to his chest for a moment, the rim depositing a smudge on his white shirt. Given my line of work, I couldn't help fixating on it. East's eyes followed mine. In an attempt to brush away the dirt, his heavy hand deepened the stain.

"Well, I guess this is what I get for not having a wife to properly dust my hat." East smiled off his embarrassment. "Or the means to afford a laundress as good as you."

"Where's your coach now?" Mama asked.

"Back at my cottage, ma'am. A man tires of pulling on the reins of a beast. Any day now," he continued, "I'm going to purchase a horseless. Just as soon as I earn me enough money," he said, smiling. "If you like, you can tell me at church what you decide, Carrie, about accepting my help."

"All right," I answered.

East seemed to consider putting his hat back on and then thought better of it. "Y'all have a good day." The handsome man turned on his heels and walked off the same way he had come, his bowler down at his side.

When he was well out of earshot, Teddy asked, "What do you think?"

"It would be nice," I said.

Mama put her hand on her hip. "I'll help and won't take your money for my trouble," she scoffed. "You two get on now, before you're late and in trouble with Mr. Calhoun."

CHAPTER ELEVEN

————◆————

At seven thirty sharp, Mr. Calhoun officially began the school day with three rings of his trusty bronze handbell. We lined up in order according to grade. As eighth-graders, we were last.

Mr. Calhoun touched the shoulder of the first pupil in the line of the youngest children. The little ones followed Everett Hurston's lead and filed into the schoolhouse. Mr. Calhoun waited a few moments before prompting the next group and then finally ours. Led by Zora, we entered. The younger children were all standing behind their seats and broke into applause as we entered the classroom. Our line gave way to a row. Zora glanced at me, I glanced at her, and Teddy glanced at us both. Mr. Calhoun let us have our eighth-grade moment. Then he took his place behind his lectern and nodded. "You may take your seats," he said.

Mr. Calhoun bade us good morning and said he expected excellence from every single one of us, especially his most senior pupils.

Every grade was to begin the day with reading and handwriting, followed by mathematics and history. Geography was after recess. He also assigned sets of chores to each grade on a rotating basis.

Morning and lunch of our first day sped by. During recess, our classmates bombarded Zora with questions about the grave robbery. It didn't matter to them that Teddy and I were also eyewitnesses; they did the natural thing and looked to a storyteller for the details.

"Zora, what did the grave look like?" asked Prat Jacobs, a caramel-skinned sixth-grader whose smooth face was punctuated by a chin dimple. "Was it just a hole in the ground or was there fire shooting out of it, like a portal to Hell?"

Zora hesitated, both impressed by Prat's imagination and a little frightened of it. "No. It was just a hole in the ground." Uncharacteristically, Zora kept to the facts. She knew that, once she started to tell the tale, she might let slip too much about our last actual encounter with Chester Cools.

Percy Bland, somehow sensing this, asked, "That last time you saw him, did you think Mr. Cools was really going to shoot you?" His interest in violence far outweighed his dismay at it. Masses of loose, shiny ringlets mixed with corkscrew curls crowned the boy's moon-shaped face. A transplant from Georgia, Percy lived in Blue Bay with his mama. Last year, when Mr. Calhoun had Percy introduce himself on the first day of school, Percy included the information that his daddy was dead. Sometimes that really meant that your daddy was dead, like mine. Sometimes it meant that you didn't know who your daddy was but did know that he was white. In Percy's case, we suspected the latter.

Zora answered honestly. "I don't know what Mr. Cools was going to do. But I doubt he had it in him to shoot a couple of kids," she finished, in defense of the old man.

"Somebody gets hurt in Eatonville and you're there, Zora. Always," Stella Brazzle remarked petulantly from a game of jacks with Joanne, Nella, and Hennie: the Brazzle gang.

Then Stella spoke to the entire schoolyard, beginning to recount Zora's crimes of presence and proximity: "Remember that fella Ivory, whose body was discovered at the railroad tracks without a head? Turns out, he was a friend of Zora's! And remember when Mr. Polk got stabbed a while back? Guess who was involved? Zora, that's who. And maybe Mr. Cools wasn't as crazy as everyone thinks. My father said Mr. Cools had barricaded his door. And no wonder! He was probably trying to keep Zora out! He was trying to keep away from her curse! She's cursed, y'all, cursed!"

Murmurs and gasps rippled across the schoolyard. Zora marched over to Stella's cabal and scooped up the scattered metal jacks. Silent, seething, Zora heaved the mass of jacks into Stella's face. Stella's head jerked, and she immediately cupped her nose with her hands.

Neat streams of blood, like skinny crimson ribbons, ran between her fingers. "Aaah!" she screeched.

Stella's yowl unofficially closed recess. Bell in hand, Mr. Calhoun sped outside.

"My goodness! Stella, what happened?"

"Zora Hurston!" Stella roared. "That evil girl tried to kill me!"

CHAPTER TWELVE

Mr. Calhoun sent Stella home to her father teary-eyed and pitiful, apparently absolved of wrongdoing. Zora, on the other hand, was sentenced to a catalog of chores.

During recess for a whole month, she was to wipe down slate boards and wash windows, shine the tongue-and-groove schoolhouse floor with linseed oil, scrub the cloakroom shelf where the lunch pails were kept, and tend to both the girls' and boys' privies. I felt horrible. Our schoolmaster said his eighth-graders had acted like a mob when he expected us to behave like role models. He also announced his intention to call on each of our families formally. Unsurprisingly, the Hurston house was the first stop on Mr. Calhoun's tour. He had already been invited there for supper that evening to celebrate the start of the new school year. It wasn't Reverend Hurston's backhand I feared most on Zora's behalf. It was Mrs. Hurston's disappointment.

In an offering of moral support, I waited for Zora to finish her first afternoon of detention. Teddy would have stayed, but he had chores back at home. Since Mr. Calhoun had barred me from helping Zora, on top of waiting alone, that hour I did nothing worked me over good. I think Stella's curse speech, given a little time, had worked Zora over as well. She set out from her first day of detention determined to find out once and for all what was behind all that had happened to Chester Cools.

Zora rushed out of the schoolhouse and quickly through the schoolyard. "Let's go!" she said.

"Go where?" I asked. "Where are we going?" Zora had been having a conversation in her head. Her feet were in on it, too. I had a lot of catching up to do.

"To Mr. Cools's place!" Zora said, exasperated, as if it should have been obvious.

I startled. "Why would we go back there?"

"Remember the story Old Lady Bronson told us?" she said. "In that story, all the zombies had been slaves once. Well, slaves have masters. What if Chester didn't dig himself out? What if his old master did? Maybe that's who he was afraid of that day we saw him."

"No! You sound like the boys at recess today!" I protested. "If Mr. Cools were immortal, that would mean he was either God or the devil. I just can't believe a poor old man with only a half-blind mule, a one-room cabin, and a peach tree to his name was either of those things. I can't! Neither should you!"

"I don't think he's God or the devil. I think Mr. Cools is something else."

"You mean *was* something else," I corrected.

"No. I mean *is*," Zora answered. "And the secret to his immortality could be in his house!"

"Mr. Cools died, Zora," I said. "He died. What could there be at his house that would change that fact?"

"Some proof or some sign of the thing that keeps him alive!"

Zora was incomprehensible to me at that moment. She was hopeful, manically so. At first, profound frustration filled me, but that was quickly overtaken by a grief so strong it was physical.

This was really about her mother.

Since the grave robbery, an image had been flashing in my mind over and over: the body of Mr. Cools being thrown into the box of a cheap wagon with less care than a sack of potatoes or squash. Worse, his body always landed atop another body—my daddy's.

So restarted my well-worn roll of questions: Had some drunken fool pushed my father into a ditch? Had he gotten into an accident in some remote field, and no one around knew who he was, let alone how to find his family? Or did he eat some food that had spoiled, tried to sleep it off, but never awoke? Thinking him lazy or drunk instead of worthy of a second look, the camp packed up, moved on, and left my father in desperate need of help or already dead.

Of course, I would have done anything to save my own father if I could. And, in my imagination, I did. No matter how many different versions of my father's resurrection I told myself over the years, however, they inevitably led back to the most probable fact of all: death.

And suddenly I knew what was driving Zora, what

this was really all about. And I could not let her face it alone.

"I'll go with you to Mr. Cools's house," I said. "I'll go." In some form or another, Death and Zora were formally introducing themselves to each other.

CHAPTER THIRTEEN

The broken window on Mr. Cools's cabin had been covered with a flimsy yellowing sheet. The turnip patch had withered. The split-rail yard that had seemed too big for one mule now appeared too small for any mules without Girly there to recommend it. And Mr. Cools's famous peach tree hung so heavily with fruit that a few branches had snapped. Large fuzzy globes rotted, scattershot, on the ground.

"I thought that the tree would be picked clean," I said. People and animals don't agree on much in frontier country except for what's safe to eat. Apparently, the fruit on Mr. Cools's tree had gone from universally coveted to universally cursed.

Zora approached the door to the cabin, turned the knob, and pushed. It was open. I stepped in beside her, and we peered around the room. A cot was posted against one wall, and a cooking hearth and a makeshift sink stood against the other. Drab, commonplace. Right inside the door were the things that Mr. Cools had used to build his barricade: the chair, the table, the trunk.

"I don't know what I thought we'd find here," Zora said in self-reproach. The question was more for herself than for me, so I said nothing. "I'm sorry, Carrie," she said, "let's get out of here. I'm sorry."

We turned to go. That's when I saw the obvious. "What about this thing?" I asked, tapping the trunk with my foot.

It was as if we were seeing the trunk for the first time. "My, this thing is grand-looking," said Zora. "Nicer than that toothpick coffin Mr. Cools was buried in."

Tooled leather straps straddled the rich oak steamer like a harness. The brass corner bumps and the silver lock plate and the draw bolts looked fit for a suit of armor. Zora unhitched the lock plate and began to lift the lid, then abruptly let it drop closed with a bang.

"It's too cramped and dark in here to see," she said, grabbing one handle. I grabbed the other handle, and we dragged the trunk out over the cabin's threshold. In the sunlight, the steamer's metal accents gleamed and floral engravings were now visible on the lock plate. Zora lifted the domed lid all the way open this time. My mouth and nose were filled with the odors of metal and rust and ancient wood and blood. An ivory brocade cloth covered in tea stains was the first thing we saw. Zora lifted the fabric from its resting place. Dust plumed. I choked and coughed. Unaffected, Zora knelt before the trunk. It was a few moments before I could kneel beside her.

It was a few more before I figured out what we were looking at: a camera. A metal cylinder jutted out of a wooden box like a tentacle topped off with an eyeball. Mahogany and rectangular, the elegant machine practically stretched the entire length of the steamer. It was strange enough that Mr. Cools had owned such an ornate trunk. It was stranger yet for him to own a camera. Cameras were expensive, celebrated, rare objects. White photographers didn't often allow Negroes into their studios. Negro photographers traveled to satisfy the demand. As a photographer in Eatonville, Mr. Cools could have been one of the most prosperous men in town. He chose not be. Why?

"Do you think it was his?" I asked. "Do you think he knew how to use it?"

"Maybe." Zora reached inside the steamer. "There's a lot more stuff in here besides." She pulled out a handful of tintypes and separated them into a few random piles on the ground.

The picture leading the first set was of a wedding party posed before a stone church. Under that was a portrait of the newlyweds at the altar. The groom stood with one hand possessively placed on his seated bride's shoulder. A portrait of the bride alone followed. Her face was dead center, and the white frilly collar sprouting around her chin gave her an air of frivolity her eyes didn't brook.

"Goodness," I said, "we worked ourselves up over an old camera and some pictures. Over nothing."

"Look at this one." Zora held up the next picture in the series, a landscape. A grassy expanse dried and hardened into a rocky sea cliff. The sepia sky, at the horizon, seemed to drown in a black sea. And on the cliff, which drew to a sharp edge, the lines and the placing of the rocks formed something that resembled a contorted face. Zora laid the portrait of the bride beside the sea cliff. "Do you see that?" she asked, pointing to the rock and then back to the bride. "It looks like her. You think someone carved her face there?"

"It's possible," I answered. "It could also be an optical illusion." I liked the way those words sounded and was surprised to find they were mine. So was Zora.

"You sound just like Teddy," she said, and picked up another group of pictures. Initially anyway, she was disappointed by one of a large brick house with lovely wide eaves and ornamental brackets. The climate pictured looked cooler than anywhere in Florida. Groves of mature, bare trees stood in the spacious front and side yards. A coal-black lawn jockey stood beside the gate of a white picket fence.

The next picture was of a white family at the house. It must have been spring or summer; leaves cloaked the trees. A heavyset woman and a bearded man sat in chairs while a girl and boy who looked a flutter younger than us stood behind them. The woman's eyes were set close, and her mouth was a bow. The man's heavy brows and beard veiled much of his face. The boy was looking far off at something beyond the camera. The girl was staring deep into the camera's mechanical eye. On the porch, several yards behind the family grouping, two black people lingered: a woman with a broom and a boy about Teddy's height.

In the next one, the bearded man was gone and the lady of the house posed on the steps with the girl and boy. The rippling force of the woman's sorrow swept her face up into her wide sunken eye sockets. The son's unfocused gaze hardened to match the flat, iron gray of his Confederate uniform. All the while, the girl had ripened. Undertones brightened her now-plump face. More than healthy, she looked beautiful. The black people remained in the background, on the porch. The kerchiefed woman's shoulders were gathered up into her neck as if from the chill of a prolonged fright. The boy was a man now, and his gaze bore into the family's backs. He ached to express something.

In the next picture, that same young man hung from a sycamore in that same yard, his body streaked with blood, tattered clothes clinging to his body. The straightest, most horrible line I ever saw in my life was that hangman's rope stretching from a thick branch of the tree all the way down to the back of the man's head, where it neatly coiled around his neck like a rattler. Below the effigy, six men wearing Confederate uniforms stood in a half ring, smiling. My imagination colored their eyes tidewater green.

The next image, for a few seconds, offered respite. A small butter-skinned black boy in a striped shirt stood holding a large book to his chest. Behind him a pair of large doors, partially open, could be seen. Through the gap, one could spot a white square of tablecloth and the dark head of someone sitting at the table. I focused on that head and gasped when I recognized it, the black in the breach. The faceless, living darkness from my nightmare was seated at that table. Spellbound, Zora touched the blot, then quickly pulled her fingers away. Her fingertips were stained with a blue-black stickiness, like the slime of a dark worm. Zora flung the photo away. It landed, soundlessly, amid the rotting fruit on the ground.

We fled, but in our bones, we felt that those scenes stamped on tin still had business with us.

CHAPTER FOURTEEN

The front door was open. Mrs. Hurston stood at the mirror in the hazy foyer, pinning a silver comb in her hair. Suddenly she bent over and had a coughing fit. Her head jerked and the silver comb glinted like a shooting star. Zora hurried in to her mother's side. Sarah rushed from the kitchen. "Mama, let us help you. Mama, sit. What are you doing up? Mama, Mama, Mama . . ."

"It's just the smoke from the solarium," Mrs. Hurston managed, trembling. "Your father's in there with Mr. Calhoun and East. Really, I'm all right," she said. "I am." She wasn't all right. Nothing was. Then Lucy Hurston spotted the black stain on Zora's hand.

"What's that?" Her eyes jumped from Zora's hand to Zora's face. She took in Zora's unkempt hair, her sweaty dress, and crooked socks—one up at her knee, the other bunched down around her ankle. Mrs. Hurston looked to my equally disheveled appearance for confirmation that something was amiss.

"What's that on your hand?" she asked again. "Whatever happened?"

Zora told the truth and lied at the same time: "This is just some smudged ink," she said, holding up her hand. "We've been running and it's hot, so the sweat must have made it run. That's all."

Sarah, probably sensing that her little sister was holding something back and wanting her to keep it that way, interrupted: "The both of you go wash up for supper, please."

The interruption worked. "Yes," Mrs. Hurston said. "Go clean up. We have guests."

In the washroom, Zora cleaned the ink off her hand and we put ourselves together as best we could.

Back in the kitchen, we found Sarah glancing from platter to platter on the sideboard, making sure the meal was ready to put on. She was wearing an ivory frock fitted at the waist, and her rum-colored face glowed. Her dark eyes—intelligent, attentive, steady—were also sweet. Her spiraled braid, piled high and neat, resembled a black blossom. Sarah might have been in her own home, but she had appointed herself with style and grace enough for a fine dining room, in Savannah, in Charleston, in New Orleans.

She handed me a platter of okra. "Carrie, please take this out to the table. I'm going to get everyone. We're ready."

Reverend Hurston delivered a short prayer. We took our seats and he served himself first. East sat beside Sarah. Everett glared at East. At the other end of the table, Mrs. Hurston passed the okra without serving herself any. Zora spooned some off her plate onto her mother's.

"Try and eat something, Mama. Please," Zora begged.

John Hurston derided his daughter. "I don't know why you think you can tell anyone anything. Not with the way you bought yourself a month's worth of detention on the first day of school. I'd like to put my foot in your behind when I think of the way I'm gonna have to grovel at Brazzle's feet tomorrow when he pays your mother a house call."

Mr. Calhoun flashed a look at Zora, then spoke up,

clearly disapproving of John Hurston's tone: "I took no pleasure in punishing you today," Mr. Calhoun said to Zora. "However, I do want to impress upon you that it's never in your best interest to act beneath your character. In fact, I would say striking someone and groveling are two types of behavior that are beneath anyone's character. Anyone's."

East smiled goofily. "Not mine. Some days I strike my horse." No one thought his joke was funny. Sarah looked a little embarrassed. "Other days I grovel at her nose, feeding her handful after handful of oats. I've saved enough money though that I could purchase two motor carriages if I sent her to the glue factory." East's eyes landed on Mr. Hurston. "My business has been going so well that I can now afford to buy an automobile."

"Oh, has it?" Mr. Hurston asked, genuinely interested—not in East, but in money.

East's gray-and-white-striped shirt narrowed his chest into a washboard, straight and strong. "Sir, it has," he declared proudly.

East's bland talk had helped to settle Zora. Respect for her schoolmaster, if not remorse for her actions, had likely weakened the wall of defenses she had erected against her father. I watched Mr. Hurston observe this. Any consolation Zora felt encouraged him to keep picking at her.

"You didn't make Stella feel bad about what she said," he sneered. "You made Stella Brazzle dislike you more. I can't say that I blame the poor girl."

"Stella said that Mr. Cools should have shot me, Daddy!" Zora snapped back. "I'm in no competition for her affection!"

"You will be tomorrow. When Doc Brazzle comes by here, you're going to say you're sorry."

Fury lowered Zora's voice: "I'm not apologizing for anything. Stella deserved what she got. What I don't deserve is you taking her side over mine."

"Right. I'm on her side." Mr. Hurston laughed balefully. "I just provide the clothes on your back and the food in your stomach. Attacking the doc's daughter while your mama is sick is a new low, even for you."

Mrs. Hurston looked far from well. She looked like she could cut somebody, namely her husband. "There's no need for Brazzle tomorrow or anytime," she said. "I trust Old Lady Bronson. She's the one with my confidence."

"Why?" His wife's bias, more than her animosity

toward him, wounded Mr. Hurston's pride. "Brazzle attended medical school. Where'd Old Lady Bronson learn? In the slave quarters?" He mocked the very ancestors that helped to make his prosperous life possible.

"I've attended college." Mr. Calhoun wasn't boasting. Rather, he was presenting facts. "Yet Lucia Bronson has the only complete set of natural science encyclopedias I've ever seen in my life, including alchemical texts. There are many ways to acquire an education, a meaningful education, outside of formal schooling."

The schoolmaster had scored one on the man of God: Mr. Hurston had never spent one hour in a schoolhouse as a student. He'd grown up the illegitimate, illiterate, half-white stepson of a coal-black, jealous sharecropper, who paradoxically whipped John Hurston out of his own self-loathing. Since his stepfather wanted him beat down so badly, John Hurston figured he had it within himself to stand tall and reach high. And he was loved tenderly by his mother. John's confidence propelled him to seek life outside the town his white father owned and beyond the patch of dusty rocks his stepfather rented.

In the next county, across the creek, colored folks

thrived. There, John Hurston began his search for prosperity, at Notasulga Baptist. Colored with some means and valid insurance policies worshipped there, including the Potts family, who owned ten acres out-right. A man earns credibility when a smart, pretty girl with plenty of choices casts her lot with him. So it went with John Hurston.

Smaller than the other girls, Lucy Potts strutted and sang in the choir. Brighter than the other girls, she taught Sunday school. John Hurston dutifully courted the thirteen-year-old with candy, dolls, and ribbons. In return, Lucy Potts did much more for John Hurston than hail from a successful family. At Sunday school, she taught him how to read. Her instruction had made the man he would become possible.

"Every town and every village is its own school," John Hurston said defensively. "The lessons I get from them educates me on what matters most: what's in people's hearts. Otherwise I don't know what I'd have to say on Sundays. Lord God knows I miss the road."

"When we got married," Lucy reminisced, calling up for her husband a picture of their youth, "I told you, John — and I know you remember it, too —

You cross the creek, that's good and all. But what you gonna do after that?"

In answer, Mr. Hurston counted the feathers in his cap. "Honey, I moved us to Eatonville. I became a carpenter, then a reverend. I've gained the respect of believers across three states. I have hundreds, maybe thousands, of parishioners. What more," he asked, "is there left for me to do besides stay black and die?"

"A vigil for Terrace Side," Lucy Hurston said. "That one's for you and only you."

"Yes. It's a shame that it has to be done at all," he said.

"But there's more than that that needs doing," she said.

"But I'm only one man," John Hurston answered, smiling.

"That might be," his wife replied, "but you're the right man."

"The right man for what?"

"Joe Clarke's third six-year term is up in a month," Lucy Hurston answered. "He's been mayor since the incorporation of Eatonville eighteen years ago. In those eighteen years, Eatonville has never had an election because no one has ever run against Joe. I think the town is ready for a change. You're ready. Run for mayor, John."

Lucy Hurston rightly suspected her husband would do for the town what she could not depend on him to do for the family. Stay put. He leaned back, giddy at the possibility of a new triumph. Everett looked on blankly as if fair weather were being discussed. Sarah's smile stretched from her mother's end of the table to her father's. East's face mirrored Sarah's. The effort made the young handsome man look alien. Zora alone scowled, stunned. She had never much cottoned to living in her father's house. How could she bear to live in her father's town? Mr. Calhoun, our teacher, understood that, and more.

"After the killing of Terrace Side and the desecration of Chester Cools's grave, Eatonville doesn't know which way is up," the schoolmaster said, sad and adamant. "I think prayer and coming together as a community would help everyone settle. An election will only cause more upheaval, the last thing this town needs. And the last thing, John, it sounds like you truly want," Mr. Calhoun reminded him. "The job of mayor is a long way from your beloved road. A long way."

John Hurston took the schoolmaster's comment

to heart. "I was a long way from home when Terrace Side was lynched," he said. "I don't know if anybody could have kept that man alive, but I would bet my bottom dollar that a man worth his gaiters could have kept some of those boys from terrorizing us here in Eatonville. If I had been home"—John Hurston said the words I suspected Mrs. Hurston might have whispered in his ear on a recent night, all too knowledgeable of her worsening condition—"things might have gone differently."

The crest of John Hurston's thoughts peaked and crashed, and a jubilant smile lit his face. John Hurston loomed very large. The table grew very small. He had decided. He would run for mayor, not run from home. John Hurston was an enviable man because he was a satisfied one.

"With my strength and God's," Lucy Hurston purred artfully, "you're going to win."

CHAPTER FIFTEEN

I awoke before Mama the next morning, dressed, left her a note, and tiptoed out into the dawn. Aiming to pick up the load from Mrs. Hopson's, which I did twice monthly, and get back home to soak the sheets before half past six, I took a short-cut through the tall grass, where my feet got wet and my shins ran slimy with dew. Approaching the pickup point, hungry, sodden, and tired, I could tell from the sky's color that the five o'clock hour had not yet passed. A band of red lined the horizon. Before long, red would become purple and purple would change to blue.

Steps from the Hopson gate where the bundle had been left for me, I began to hobble in my damp socks and wet boots. The basket handle chafed my left hand. My empty stomach bleated and cramped. I arrived home nearly an hour later than I had intended, ready to eat three meals and drop back into bed.

Teddy, who was waiting on my steps, had another idea: "Your mama went to Sanford to drop some thread by a friend," he said. "Change your clothes. We can still make it to school on time."

I limped to my washing barrel and carefully placed the basket of linens beside it. Both my left hand and the blisters on my feet burned angrily. I didn't think I could go to school, at least not in a hurry. "Go without me," I said. "I'm not feeling too well."

"What's the matter?" Teddy crossed the yard. "Where have you been?"

"At Mrs. Hopson's in Maitland," I answered, hobbling toward the steps to remove my boots. Teddy helped me and I was able to stand upright. As I began to untie my laces, Teddy noticed my hand and gently stopped me from using it.

"My goodness," he said, holding my wrist. "Is that a rope burn?"

"It's from the basket," I said. "My hands are

so dry from the lye, I guess the skin just gave way." Teddy gingerly touched the edges of the gray blister. I tried not to flinch. I didn't succeed. The morning had been challenging, but the last couple of weeks, from Terrace Side to Chester Cools, only added to my feelings of fragility. And there was the most recent headline news that John Hurston was running for mayor. But the thing that really got under my skin about that was the idea that two dead men and a sick woman were some of the reasons Zora's father might actually be able to win.

Teddy stood and shifted his weight uncomfortably. He studied my hand, and his lovely lips flattened into a reedy line. "It's so strange, Carrie. But your blister . . . it's like so many that were on Mr. Cools."

"What?" Chilly prickles shot up my neck. The sensation instantly turned down the heat on my wounds. Like little arctic streams, sweat ran down my skin.

Teddy grimaced. "You know I helped Doc Brazzle prepare his body for burial." I nodded. Teddy continued, "Mr. Cools had many, many wounds. Some had healed. Others hadn't. None of them were recent, but a few of them were fresh somehow. It was the strangest thing. Scary, actually. I asked Doc Brazzle about it."

"What did he say?"

"That he was surprised Chester hadn't died long ago. The man had gunshot wounds on his torso. A bullet still lodged in one. I can't imagine how he survived the infection. And you know those folds of skin that old folks and babies have under their necks?"

"Yeah." I gulped.

"Mr. Cools had an ear-to-ear blister there, fresh as the one on your hand. The worse kind of burn—a burn that never healed."

A sudden pulse of fear enraged me. "Why did so many bad things happen to him? Why?" I cried.

"I don't know, Carrie. I don't," Teddy admitted, suddenly whey-faced and sweaty. "And those bad things that happened to Mr. Cools left their mark on his body." Teddy blinked and a drop of sweat rolled over his eyelid. "Just like the grave robbery and the lynching of Terrace Side have left their mark on our town."

Another drop of sweat made an ashy path down his face. He wiped it away with a dull slap. His movements were slowing; his speech was sluggish. Then his eyes rolled back, his knees buckled, and it happened so fast that there was no time to try to catch him.

"Teddy!" I cried as he collapsed. "Teddy!"

CHAPTER SIXTEEN

s I struggled to lift him, I prayed. As I dragged
him up the steps onto the porch and into the
house, I prayed. As I laid him on my cot, I
prayed that he would awaken, that he would speak,
that he would return to himself, to me. *Dear God, heal
Teddy. Dear God, please keep Teddy here with me.*

A glass of water sat on the dresser, and I rushed it
to him, propping up his head and wetting his lips. He
murmured; he struggled to open his eyes but couldn't,
not completely. *Breathe. Breathe. Dear God, let him breathe.*
When I pulled my hand away, it was streaked with
blood. Had he been hit, cut? I searched his head and

neck. Where was the wound? I'd use cotton and lace from Mama's sewing table to bind it. I'd dress his wound in finery. *Where is the wound? God, help me find the wound. I beg You.* Then my own hand came into sharp relief. The blister on my hand had popped. The blood was mine. My wound was weeping for Teddy. Then I felt a strange pressure on my shoulder. *Don't look back,* I said to myself. *If you look back, Teddy will die.*

A voice spoke. My fear scrambled the words into gibberish. I could not look back. No. The pressure came again. I closed my eyes. I put my bloody hand to my face. I tasted metal, rust. The flavor of blood returned me to myself. Words again made sense. *Child, child. How long has he been like this? How long? Your hand. Your hand. Child.*

Old Lady Bronson had taken my hand into hers and was examining it while she touched Teddy's forehead. I asked, "What do you want me to do?"

"Bring me all the alcohol you've got."

Next to where the glass of water had been, we had a small bottle on the dresser. I gave it to her.

"Go to Joe Clarke's for more. Before you leave, bring me more water."

I dashed to the water barrel in the kitchen and stopped dead in front of the fat drum, frantic.

Without looking, I knew there wasn't enough in there now for a full ladle. Teddy and Micah hadn't gotten us water from the well in weeks.

I sprinted outside for my wooden laundry oar and wedged it between the five-inch limestone cap and the well lip. I took a step back, pulling the oar as steadily and with as much strength as I could. The cap dislodged some. I pulled. The sloshing sound of the water made me thirsty. Had I moved it enough? Maybe? I cranked. The bucket refused to pass. So I tugged the oar again. The pulpy stick broke off in my bloody hands. I threw it to the ground. I dug the heels of my hands into the storm-gray chunk of mountain. My hands were slick with blood. A horrible pressure ground down into my left wrist. Finally, the force of my frustration shunted the limestone. Again, I cranked. The bucket passed. I filled it and sped through the yard back to the house. Drops of my blood fell into the water.

"Tell Joe Clarke I need ice, too," Old Lady Bronson ordered. "Plenty of it."

I grabbed some lace from Mama's sewing table, wrapped my hand with it, and raced off for Mr. Clarke's. With every breath and every step, I inhaled and exhaled pain, a pain that distorted the cedars and the clearing and the forest. A pain that made it feel as though the tall grass along the roadside was bludgeoning me. A water moccasin bumped across my toes, and the tip of its hard, scaly body zapped my ankle like lightning. Heat coiled in the air. The journey felt like a fryer.

When I arrived at Joe Clarke's, a layer of red ash from the road coated my hair, my dress, my skin. I looked like I was carrying a hell inside of me and that the devil had forced me to sweat it out. I needed to say "ICE! ALCOHOL! NOW!" But the clay dust had evaporated my saliva. My journey had nearly made me mute.

Nate Landing sat on the porch railing flipping a nickel. The sight of me caused him to fumble the coin. "Somebody," he warbled. "Somebody!"

Joe Clarke appeared, followed by John Hurston and Zora. "Carrie!"

Zora charged down the stairs. Reflexively, Mr. Hurston reached out to hold her back, but she was already at my side. It was one of the few times I had seen John Hurston act protectively toward her.

Zora's eyes went from my hand to my face. I could not speak above a whisper. Zora was going to have to come very close to hear. She did.

"Fever. Teddy," I panted at her neck. "Old Lady Bronson. Sent me. Ice. Alcohol."

Joe Clarke left to tell the Bakers about Teddy. Mr. Hurston and Zora brought me home with the alcohol. When the Bakers arrived at my house, Old Lady Bronson gave out instructions. Mr. Clarke and Mr. Hurston were to get ice from a Daytona factory that sold slabs of it for rail cars and hotels. Mr. Baker was to turn Teddy over. Mrs. Baker was to stop crying and apply rubbing alcohol to Teddy's chest, back, and legs. Without a word from the roots woman, Micah got his tools from his coach and waited.

Joe Clarke and John Hurston returned with the ice. Micah sawed sheets of it from the slab. I fetched a blanket to cover the slices so Micah could crush them with a large mallet. Zora gathered pans and bowls from the kitchen that Mr. Hurston and Mr. Clarke loaded with the ice. Old Lady Bronson pulled chairs to the sides of my cot. Zora placed the bowls of ice there and Old Lady Bronson placed Teddy's hands in them for timed intervals every hour. Teddy twitched and shuddered at each treatment, but his eyes remained shut. Mr. Hurston offered what he could to the Bakers.

"Doc Brazzle is at my house right now. I'll go home and send him here. Come on, Zora."

"I can't leave," she protested.

"It's all right," I said. "My mother will be home soon. Go."

Zora's misgivings persisted. "You need help," she said. "Your hand . . ."

"Your hand?" My mother arrived and rushed through the grove of people to my side in our meager sitting room. "Dear Lord, what happened?" she asked. "What happened?"

"Oh, Mama," I cried. "Teddy's sick."

"I just saw him this morning," she said, her doubt countering her dread.

"That's when it happened."

"Your hand?" She looked at it even though she couldn't bear to.

"I got a blister from a laundry basket. Carrying Teddy and moving the well cap made it worse."

"Doc Brazzle should see the boy and that hand," Mr. Hurston said. "We better get on so I can fetch him."

"Yes," Mama answered. "Please."

Zora accepted that the will of our parents, respectively, was the best course of action. We embraced, and alongside her father, she left. The Baker men and Joe Clarke settled on the porch while Mrs. Baker remained in the bedroom with Teddy and Old Lady Bronson. Mama sat at the kitchen table with me, where time didn't exactly pass, but lurk. And Doc Brazzle, when he arrived, only made that feeling worse. He could not do more for Teddy nor my hand than Old Lady Bronson had already done.

After he examined Teddy, Doc Brazzle said, "It looks like the flu. His heart is very weak." Men in Eatonville rarely hugged, but the doctor embraced both Micah and Mr. Baker. Teddy may have been his apprentice, but it was clear the physician thought of him more like a son.

That night, no one ate and no one slept. Teddy sipped air in tiny gulps, and we sat with him in shifts. The transparency of his skin, sickly beautiful, increased under the hazy glow of the kerosene lamp. At dawn, the Baker men lifted Teddy from my cot onto a stretcher Doc Brazzle had let them borrow. They loaded him onto Micah's wagon and drove him home — taking him there, I feared, to die.

PART II

CHAPTER SEVENTEEN

In that glittering evening light unique to the month of September, a week after Teddy's collapse, John Hurston led the vigil for Terrace Side at Lake Bell. With the exception of Joe Clarke, who was in Tallahassee campaigning for the expansion, the whole town attended.

On the embankment where the doomed man had been burned, small children collected in leggy clumps under tall, slanted palms. In the water where the fugitive bled, red pennants waved atop poles representing the Father, the Son, and the Holy Ghost. Parishioners, two and three deep, waded into the water up to their waists. In a white robe, Reverend Hurston led us.

A red band anointed with oil and embroidered with a white cross graced his forehead. Gone was the black suit and the attending collars, cuffs, and pins of the pulpit. Here, in the water, the encircling robe of the Redeemer represented something beyond the sharp points of propriety and judgment. The white robe adorning John Hurston represented forgiveness, a new start.

"Good evening," John Hurston greeted the throng.

"Good evening, Reverend," the throng resounded.

"I'd like to start by speaking on how good God is, how good God has been to us here in Eatonville, and how good God is all the time. All the time!"

The crowd sounded with "Yes, sir," "Go on, now," and "Praise be to the Lord." Folks, including me, were grateful for the spectrum of comforts in our lives—from decent clothes and shelter to the safety of loved ones. But into that sense of gratitude and relief, John Hurston began to pour regret and self-incrimination. He continued: "For years, God spared us hurricane landfalls in September. For years, God sprinkled November frost in its rightful place up north. God nurtured citrus groves here in northern

Florida and grew jobs for us on and in trees. At the dozens of turpentine camps across the county, no one has been seriously injured for months. The prosperity has flowed blood-free. This has got folks to thinking that it is us, mortal men, who are responsible for the bounty. That it is us everyday folks who make life good," John Hurston paused. "The arrogance of man. The stubborn, fatal arrogance of man."

John Hurston reminded us how easy it was to take for granted conditions that were a gift, not a given; to forget that good fortune had been shared with us more than had been shaped by us.

Zora's father continued: "We, the believers, are His chosen people. And the flame of our faith is an imperiled thing. Envied by desperate men such as Terrace Side and despised by evil men, our faith is a fragile thing amid the tinder of desperate men and evil men. Our flame of faith is not to guide the sinner. Our flame of faith is for us to tend ours, nurture ours. Bertram Edges's house full of glass; Willie Mosely's broken limb; Maisie and Bynum's livestock. By the light of our neighbor's misfortunes, we better see our enemies, those who threaten the peace of God and the fragile peace of Eatonville. Our prosperity, this gift from God, did not spring from a township charter granted by the state of Florida. Our prosperity flowed from the spring of our faith, from the one true God. We pray to you, dear Lord, to help us keep what's ours safe and sound with the flame of faith."

The air was charged with something new, something prideful and protective. John Hurston held up one large Xanthus palm. "The lynching of Terrace Side is not the only wrathful event that has befallen this town of late." He paused prodigiously. "The grave robbery of Chester Cools is a horrible, horrible thing. Like the lynching of Terrace Side, the grave robbery is evil that has found us out. Even things such as these, my dear friends, happen according to His will. Why? Because we've lost our way. But in my meditation and prayer, God has shown me the path, the way. He has. God has shown me that we are a chosen people, an elect, a colored elect!"

Belief that such a path existed for us, and that it could be reclaimed, reanimated the town's faith in God, in John Hurston, and in ourselves. All was not lost. People lifted their hands up to the sky, gladdened. Tears flowed freely. Praise poured. There was a way forward, on a river of sweat and tears perhaps, but there was a way forward. There was hope.

John Hurston gave it to us with his preaching, and with an idea: "The time has arrived for the elect to take up the mantle of democracy, a true democracy, with a vote. It's time we choose for ourselves. For too long we've accepted an appointment as if it was anointed. God gave us free will. It's time we please God with the power of our choice. The elect need an election! The elect need an election! My God, the elect need an election!"

The jubilant outburst, "John Hurston for mayor!" rang out in loops over the jangle of tambourines and the pounding of drums. Too clever to announce his candidacy, John Hurston let the town announce it for him. "John Hurston for mayor! John Hurston for mayor!" His family celebrated the triumph, but no one more than Lucy.

Lucy Hurston closed her eyes, seeming to teeter between dizziness from the exertion and the spellbinding influence of her husband's power. Everett splashed and Sarah clapped. Zora moved through the crowd toward me, studying gestures and utterances of praise as she went, like the feeling of a religious experience was a scientific formula that could be activated by music and recorded and replicated for further study. "Loving Pine tomorrow morning," Zora yelled, and amid the hoots, music, and dancing, it came off as a whisper. I nodded. The vigil was the first time we had seen each other since Teddy had fallen ill. Besides everything, I missed my best friend.

The hoots softened. The music wound down. To all those in the water and on the embankment, Mr. Hurston boomed, "John the Baptist, at the river Jordan, told the crowds that 'even now the ax lies at the root of the trees. Every tree that does not produce good fruit will be cut down and thrown into the fire.' The ax was at our roots here in Eatonville for longer than we knew. We are now in the fire, the purifying fire of change. For as John the Baptist prophesied, a mightier one is coming. He is already here and 'his winnowing fan is in his hand to clear his threshing floor.' May we prove that we are not chaff. May we avoid, with the water of baptism, the 'unquenchable fire' that threatens to destroy us."

Bo Wilson, knee-deep in water, stepped out from the crowd. He stretched his arms at his sides and flung back his head. His Adam's apple quivered. Folks linked hands.

In a beautiful falsetto, Bo Wilson sang out the benediction:

"Deep river,
My home is over Jordan.
Deep river,
I want to cross over into campground.

Oh, don't you want to go
To the Gospel feast;
That Promised Land
Where all is peace?

Oh, deep river, Lord,
I want to cross over into campground.
Deep river, Lord,
Help John Hurston protect our home."

CHAPTER EIGHTEEN

The next morning, I found Zora sitting at the foot of the Loving Pine. The crate lid she used as a writing desk was in her lap, but she wasn't writing.

"I don't want to interrupt," I said.

"Do I look like I'm doing anything besides waiting for you?" Zora stood and opened her arms. "Come over here." We hugged, hard. I broke down sobbing on account of Teddy. "Carrie, Carrie, Carrie," Zora said, with such tenderness and understanding that I felt my personhood to be real and alive again for the first time in days.

We released each other. All I could say was, "It was good to see you and your mother yesterday. I've missed you."

"I doubt Mama will be able to get out of bed today." Zora shook her head in helpless anger. "She shouldn't have gone to the vigil, but she pretended to be able to do it for my father's sake." Her bitterness was palpable. "Pretending isn't helping her get well. It's not helping anyone, in fact, except my father and his bid for mayor. There's going to be a meeting at the post office about the mayoral race. My father and Joe Clarke have agreed to it."

I said, "You think your father will win, don't you?"

"I do," she answered, and the idea of her father's triumph troubled her.

Those two words again. *I do.* The future happiness that I had cavalierly assumed was mine to share with Teddy, like so many things, might never come to pass. Over the past few days, Teddy had been too ill to receive visitors and, of all things, I regretted not being able to tell him about Mr. Cools's trunk. But I could tell Zora what Teddy had said about Mr. Cools's body.

"Right before Teddy fell sick, he told me something about Chester."

"What did he tell you?"

"When he helped Doc Brazzle prepare Chester for burial, he saw that Chester's body was riddled with wounds and scars. He said there was an old bullet still in him and that there were burn marks on his throat. It looked like . . ."

"Yes?" Zora egged me on.

"It looked like people had tried to kill Mr. Cools a long time ago, even that, by rights, he should have died years earlier."

A flame of recognition blazed in Zora's eyes. "My God, Carrie!" she blurted out. "My God!" The thing that surprised me most was that I had already thought, before her, the very thing she was thinking. Only, unlike Zora, I didn't actually believe it.

Zora pieced the incredible details of the strange life and death of Chester Cools together. "I think the man that got lynched in that picture was Chester Cools. That would explain the burn scars on his neck. That was the first time he died. . . .

"And that explains his empty grave," Zora then answered her own follow-up question. "Mr. Cools has survived death twice now! I think I know something about how he did it, too."

My jaw dropped to my ankles. "You do?"

"Remember how ink from that picture in Mr. Cools' trunk got on my hand? If everything in Mr. Cools's trunk was decades old, going back to before the war, how could there have been wet ink in there? I don't think that stuff was regular ink. I think that dark sticky stuff has something to do with how Mr. Cools survived! In fact, I'm sure it does!"

My God, I thought, *my nightmare.* The roving darkness that had presented itself to me in sleep—the same darkness I had seen stare out at me from the picture—had actually reached out to touch Zora in life. Zora must have seen the loathsome revelation wash over me, because she winced. "What is it, Carrie?"

I trembled. "That dark stuff from the tintype. I've seen it before."

"You have?" Dread made Zora's voice sound hoarse.

"In a nightmare. It was coming after me. That's what I thought, anyways. Now I'm not so sure. . . ."

I knew that what I had to say next would hurt Zora, but she would have gotten it out of me, one way or another. "I think," I continued, "that the darkness was looking for you."

Zora was quiet for a moment. "Since the ink touched me," she said, "I've felt a cold numbness inside. Not all the time, but it's there, inside of me. Growing." Zora shivered contritely. I took her hand.

I wanted to say, *There's nothing inside of you truly dark. You're a seeker, Zora, a finder. But because answers are often found in the dark, in the cold, that's what you'll feel.* I wanted to say that. And I wanted to say, *We all have dark, cold places inside of us.* Instead, I closed my eyes, welling with tears, and shook my head.

"Deep down, I don't know if I'm blessed or cursed," she said, sad and weary. "My daddy says this place is for the elect, the chosen. Is that why I don't want to stay here? Because I don't belong?"

"You're a blessing," I assured Zora, "a blessing." Tears rolled down Zora's face now. I touched my forehead to hers, and we cried together. "I'm not sure the world out there deserves you," I declared. "If the town chooses your father to be mayor, I'm not sure Eatonville deserves you, either."

CHAPTER NINETEEN

In appearance and utility, Eatonville's white clapboard post office was a cross between a church and a store. Folks posted letters there, which very often felt like sending up a prayer: the letter disappeared, and responses were never guaranteed. People didn't purchase goods at the post office, but they picked up their Sears and Roebuck catalogs and parcels there, which could feel almost like an answered prayer.

Well trafficked and neutral, the post office was the perfect site for a town meeting. It didn't belong to one man, like the church seemed to belong to John

Hurston or like Joe Clarke's store belonged to Joe Clarke. The post office belonged to the town.

Mr. Johnson, as the postmaster general, accepted the duty of putting on an event where information about the upcoming election would be shared and folks could hear a few words from each of the candidates. Chairs were set up outside in front of the post office, and drums of lemonade set out on the porch to make the event a proper assembly. Two podiums were placed facing the rows of chairs. Between the podiums, a small table held a sweaty pitcher of water and two glasses.

When Micah and Daisy Baker arrived, Daisy hugged and kissed me and Mama, just like we were family. Micah looked exhausted but at ease, happy.

"I have good news, Carrie," he said. "Teddy ate a little today and is sitting up. I don't think it will be long before you can go by and see for yourself how he's doing."

"Really?" My eyes welled with tears of relief.

"Yes. And that's not all. Teddy's gonna be an uncle." Micah patted Daisy's belly then, and his obvious glee made a pun irresistible. "My wife and I have a little Baker in the oven!"

Daisy placed her hand on top of Micah's. "Oh, I love you," she cooed.

"That's wonderful!" Mama exclaimed, grasping a hand with each of hers. The gesture was as much a way of congratulating the pair as it was an attempt to touch their happiness, to claim even a small measure of it. For the first time since Teddy had taken ill, I felt like I could truly breathe again.

The news of a baby generated a sudden makeshift receiving line, folks eager to latch on to something uncontroversial, something they could all easily agree on.

Joe Clarke joined in, shaking Micah's hand and embracing Daisy.

"I hear your little brother's much better," Mr. Clarke said to Micah.

"Yes," Micah said warmly. "My parents are more grateful to you than their worry has allowed them to say. Thank you so much for the steady stream of supplies."

"I'm glad that Teddy's improved." Mr. Clarke barely paused to glance at me before saying, "He's mighty important to some very special people in this town."

Austin Johnson walked among the gathering folk like a nervous host. His glasses kept slipping down his sweaty nose. The sound of an approaching engine got everyone's attention. John Hurston had arrived, chauffeured by his eldest son in a shell-white horseless, open-roofed and gleaming. Mr. Hurston exited the grand vehicle jauntily, knocked on its shiny hood with a friendly fist, and then surveyed the scene.

Where had such a fine horseless come from? Was John Hurston suddenly rich? With a proud, wide-legged stance, he let the grand machine transform him from the Eatonville man we thought we knew into the type of worldly man men aspire to be.

Joe Clarke ambled up the center aisle to stand behind one of the two podiums. John Hurston's gaze met him there. An uncommonly decent man, Joe Clarke showed common courtesy.

"Hello, John," he said.

"Why, hello to you, Joe." John Hurston strutted up to the other podium, knocked on it like he had the gleaming horseless, then gazed skyward, as if he were delivering up a prayer. Then he slowly promenaded around the makeshift arena. We surveilled John Hurston surveilling us.

Lucy Hurston broke the spell by leading her

children to the seats Austin Johnson had reserved for them in the front row. John Hurston finally took his place behind his podium. Mr. Johnson adjusted his glasses again before calling, "Take your seats, folks. Please, take your seats. We're going to begin."

Folks shuffled about and parked their behinds. Others settled silently where they were situated. Before long, an assembly of upright backs and attentive eyes had composed itself. The town's entire civic body seemed to be holding its breath.

Mr. Johnson exhaled, perhaps on behalf of us all, and began: "Friends and fellow citizens, because we have only had one mayor in the eighteen years since our dear town was founded, the election on Saturday will be Eatonville's first. I also reckon this will be the first time many of you, including me, have voted in any election, let alone one of such consequence. Voting will take place here at the post office from sunrise through sundown. You'll be required to have your name recorded in a log in order to cast your vote, but your vote itself will be private. We flipped a coin when the candidates agreed to this presentation. John Hurston won the toss and chose to let Joe Clarke open the floor. Joe, whenever you're ready."

"Thank you, Austin," Mr. Clarke said. "And thank

you, everyone, for being here. It has been an honor to be the mayor and marshal of Eatonville for eighteen years. I'd like to share with you how Eatonville came to be, and my place in its founding.

"I grew up here in Florida, with Seminole and former slaves. We were taking care of each other, as we always had, when a white man who had fought for Lincoln's army came here and decided to make his life. That man bought the land for this place from the United States government. Our town is named for that man, Josiah Eaton.

"After the war, in the terrible aftermath of Lincoln's assassination, Mr. Eaton fought on behalf of Reconstruction, Lincoln's unfulfilled dream. We would never get the forty acres and a mule we were promised from the United States government, but Mr. Eaton set out to do right by the freedmen the only way he knew how: by giving us an opportunity to truly shape our own destinies.

"Distrustful of white men and their money, the Seminoles that were here departed for the safety and isolation of the hard-going Everglades. Mr. Eaton shocked us remaining colored folks by rejecting the proposition that he should run the place. If he had become mayor, or hadn't put the papers through to incorporate the town, this land, in the event of Mr. Eaton's death, would have been inherited by his heirs. Aware that his days were numbered, Mr. Eaton, in the spirit of Reconstruction and his radical Republican roots, committed his legacy to the public good, not private gains. Mr. Eaton passed on before Eatonville celebrated its first birthday. And in the eighteen years that I've led this town since, like Eatonville itself, I've belonged to you, the people."

If there were any sort of rules to this public encounter, John Hurston had no intention of following them. He pounced.

"Wouldn't you agree that eighteen years is a long time, Joe, to heap praise on a white man?"

"Before Eatonville was a place on a map, or a place in all of our hearts," Mr. Clarke countered, "it was the precious idea of a noble man committed to justice."

"That's the problem." Mr. Hurston did more than sharpen his knife; he thrust it. "People are what matter, not ideas! How does your plan to expand the town of Eatonville expand the people of Eatonville? I don't see it. I do see how it might expand you! I'll give it to you, Joe—your ambition helped this town get its start. But that same ambition could be what's now threatening it. . . . Terrace Side was lured here by Eatonville's promise of invincibility, but he was followed here by lynch men who want to punish Eatonville for daring to exist and now to grow. Your ambition also couldn't protect sacred ground from grave robbers or bring those resurrection men to justice. What is it your ambition can do for us today? Tell me. What is your ambition doing now besides wreaking havoc?"

An uncomfortable silence followed this condemnation, but I saw contempt bloom on my own mother's face. She despised the reverend. He offended her Christian sense of right and wrong, of conscience. Mama had said she would have taken Terrace Side in if he had come to our door. Her expression announced that, given the chance, she would just as readily run John Hurston out of town.

Joe Clarke thundered, "You give strife a helping hand when you refuse to help people! I thought you were a reverend, open and generous. In reality, you're a wrongheaded guard, amoral and mean!" At that line, my mother spontaneously clapped and called out, "Get 'im, Joe!"

Willie Mosely responded, "All right, Joe! All right!" John Hurston tensed.

Joe Clarke kept up his battle cry: "I believe that what happened with Terrace Side has only deepened my resolve on the soundness of expansion. Why would we shut our doors when the best way to protect ourselves is to grow, bigger and stronger, when how we ensure our survival as a place of promise and hope is to open our doors wider, to fortify ourselves by union and communion?"

Looking around at the faces of the crowd gathered, I didn't see clear signs that Mr. Clarke was winning anyone over.

"What makes Eatonville great," Joe Clarke continued, "is that, here, black people in a black town treat black people as we should be treated everywhere: as human beings! I want to expand this town so we can give more black women, more black men, more black children, more black babies, the opportunity to live as human beings—and the right to succeed or fail according to the quality of their efforts, not the color of the skin they were born in.

"You all know too well that no colored man in America can pursue and arrest a white man. You all know that the crime of the grave robbery, if I had pushed it, would have given whites a reason to murder me. Not that they needed another one, since running this town for eighteen years has been reason enough, I'm sure."

John Hurston flashed a barbarous smile. "But you're still here, aren't you? You've survived."

"Yes, I've survived," Mr. Clarke conceded, "but more importantly, this *town* has survived precisely because I have conducted Eatonville's business under the rule of law. As flawed as it may be, the law is why Eatonville can and does exist. As far as I can figure it, the only way forward is to continue to use the law to argue for and achieve equality under it."

The laws of white folks as being the *only way* is what frustrated, frightened folk chafed at. John Hurston capitalized on this. "And just where is God's law in all of this, Joe? Not once have I heard you mention God's holy protection, God's law. Through this town's recent misfortunes, I believe God has made clear to us that obedience to the ways and laws of white men—I daresay, your cowardice—will be our undoing. Your faith in the white man's law is a curse, Joe—a curse we can finally throw off by voting you out of office. It's time for a new leader. It's time to abandon the destructive path of ambition and to reacquaint ourselves with the path of humility!"

Zora jumped from her seat. She had lived in her father's house. She would not live in her father's Eatonville. "Mr. Clarke is not a coward!" she objected. "And what do you even know about fear and courage, Daddy? You weren't even here!" she reprimanded him. "Your own family had to fend for themselves! We did, too, with Joe Clarke's help. He was there when a fugitive was on the loose. He was there when a bloodthirsty mob came through our town and into our houses. He was there when poor Chester Cools disappeared from his grave, a zombie unable to rest."

There was an audible gasp from the assembly, murmurings of puzzled confusion. John Hurston, maybe not sure he had heard correctly, shot Joe Clarke a look. Joe Clarke hung his head. Zora, instead of taking her father down a notch, had served him, at last, the perfect ammunition to publicly denounce her and Joe Clarke.

Shock at the realization of what she had just done stiffened Zora's limbs. The life temporarily went out of her eyes.

"Oh, my child," Mr. Hurston said. "Child of my flesh, but not of my spirit. You've been raised up, not on my knee like the rest of my children, but on the front porch of a merchant. You have rejected the love and guidance of a Christian household and embraced, instead, the superstitious nonsense of gossips, busybodies, and witch doctors."

Mr. Hurston now looked directly at Joe Clarke. "What's this about you seeing Chester Cools rise from the grave like a zombie?"

Mr. Clarke took a breath, knowing that it would take all the oratorical skill and patience he had to undo the slander that Reverend Hurston spoke aloud. "I did not see Chester Cools rise from the grave. Chester Cools was not a zombie."

Zora looked at Joe, wounded and betrayed. Joe avoided her eyes.

"I've known Chester since the beginnings of this town," he said. "For as long as I've known him, Chester insisted that he was . . . that he wasn't . . . that he was unnatural. He thought he had died once, a long time ago, hanging from a tree, but had been brought back to life. Of course, I knew that to be impossible but didn't press the matter, concerned as I was with how Chester might be treated if that sort of thing were spread around.

"I believe that he must have said something about

zombies to Zora recently. His ravings," Joe Clarke continued sadly, "are now threatening to destroy his memory."

John Hurston unleashed his scorn. "Why would you think for a moment that any of us would ever have believed this nonsense about Chester? You think we're children in this town. Always have. Unlike my poor, ignorant daughter, your neighbors are children of God. We know of a greater power than Joe Clarke and put our faith in Him. We always have. We always will. I believe this town is through with you, Joe Clarke," John Hurston delivered calmly.

"That's for the people of Eatonville to decide," Joe Clarke said quietly, but I could tell he knew that the outcome had already been decided.

All this time, Zora was still standing numb, her eyes distant, already an exile far from home.

CHAPTER TWENTY

The next morning, since I couldn't use both of my hands to carry it, Mama loaded the small pot of broth I made for Teddy into a wagon Zora and I had used to gather sticks when we were little. From my house to the Baker place was either a twenty-minute walk through the woods or a fifteen-minute walk along the road. Having learned that every minute counted where Teddy was concerned, I took the road.

Beneath a gauzy sky speckled blue, the morning was cool and fine. Situated near the road, a brick-red sign with white lettering announced the Baker place: RUBY STRETCH.

In an offering to nature Herself, Mrs. Baker had named the farm for the color of their first successful crops: radishes and rutabagas. The name stuck, even once root vegetables were no longer the foundation of the family's business. *Ruby* was also a nod to the truest treasure in the Baker household: the lifeblood in their veins, the family itself.

Mr. Baker was not only the most prosperous farmer in Eatonville, but probably one of the most successful farmers, black or white, in north Florida. Mr. Baker had cottoned to plants the same way his son Teddy had cottoned to animals. Mr. Baker first gardened outside his grandmother's clapboard shack when he was a boy. Before long he worked as a hired farmhand. After years of saving, he became a farm owner himself. The independence allowed him to experiment with seed grafting. Eventually, his efforts paid off tenfold. Mr. Baker invented a new strain of wheat-rye, as hardy as it was tasty and filling. Livestock favored it. Mr. Baker supplied farmers from California to Iowa with seed. His business thrived.

Then the return-of-payment demands started arriving. Some of his seed packages had never been delivered to the purchasers; others had been delivered empty. Mr. Baker suspected the post office in

Maitland of sabotage. Some white farmers, learning of his tremendous success, were jealous and had devised a plan to destroy Ruby Stretch without pulling a trigger or lighting a match. Mr. Baker doubted that the post offices in Orlando or Jacksonville would be any better. So he hatched an ingenious plan, one that would both improve Eatonville and secure his seed business. He asked Joe Clarke to petition the government for a post office of Eatonville's own. Mr. Clarke filed the necessary paperwork and Eatonville got its very own federal building.

Mr. Baker came down the path to meet me. A tall, brown-skinned man with a handsome, cinnamon-freckled face, he wore denim overalls over a white shirt and sported a pair of silver spectacles.

"Hello," he said. "Micah came back on home after the gathering at the post office yesterday evening and said that we should expect you today. I see he wasn't wrong."

"I was the wrong one, sir," I readily admitted. "I should have looked in on Teddy sooner, much sooner."

Mr. Baker touched my arm. "You were right to stay away. You wouldn't have been settled by what you saw and it wouldn't have done Teddy any good.

The last thing in the world he wants to do is upset you. How's your hand?" he asked, pointing to the black fingerless glove I wore.

"It's better," I said. "I am, too, now, on account of your kind words."

"They're true." Mr. Baker removed his glasses, gently folded the stems, and slipped them into the front pocket of his overalls. In another time and place, Mr. Baker would have stared through microscopes at tiny cells shaped like landmasses on a secret, invisible map of life. In another time and place, he might even have accepted prizes for his discoveries. In Eatonville, Florida, in 1905, we had a different name for scientists and businessmen, especially colored ones. Back then, we called them *farmers*.

Mr. Baker accompanied me all the way up to the house. Mrs. Baker appeared behind the screen door. "Why, hello, Carrie," she said, holding the door open for me. "I think you're just the sight for sore groggy eyes someone's been yearning for."

"I have broth here," I said, retrieving the pot from the wagon.

Mrs. Baker smiled nostalgically. "Oh, I remember that old thing. You and Zora would come around here, taking turns pulling each other in that wagon.

Before I know a thing, I look out the window and what I see?" She beamed at the thought of her little boy's chivalry and selflessness: "Teddy pulling both you girls in the wagon. I never saw him sit in that thing. Not once."

"Zora and I would play with our corn-husk dolls in here, too," I added. "Teddy wore himself out pulling us and our dolls around the house, through the poplars, over to the fig trees, down to the road, and back."

"Not many of us ever really outgrow the necessity of pulling the wagon, do we, of pulling others along that need it. That's what we're all gonna have to do for Teddy to get him better." She looked at me with a sad, shepherding smile. "We're gonna have to pull him along for a bit."

I couldn't answer, knowing that if I tried to say anything, I would probably start bawling.

"Head on in, Carrie. Teddy was awake when I left him a moment ago. I'll take care of the broth."

The Bakers were the only family I knew with a two-story house. The stairs faced the front door and along the staircase hung pictures of the family. A wedding photograph of Micah and Daisy reminded me of my manners. "Congratulations on the grandbaby,"

I said, turning around. "You must be so happy."

"We are. Now, go on," she said, waving me toward the stairs. All along the wall of the staircase leading up to Teddy's bedroom, tintypes of the Baker family hung. Suddenly I couldn't bear to look at them, afraid that I might see some horrible black ink. I was most afraid that I would see it in pictures of Teddy, see it swallowing him up. I kept my eyes on my feet and silently chanted, *Teddy is better! Teddy is better! Teddy is better!* until I arrived at the top of the landing. At the end of the hallway, Teddy's door was ajar and light spilled from his room into a little flickering puddle on the floor. I knocked.

"Come in," he answered hoarsely.

I pushed the door. Teddy smiled, but his appearance took my breath away. His lips were chapped from the effects of fever. His neck sparkled with the salt left over from his sweats. The coiled hair on his arms looked like it had been scorched. The fever had burned away the final remnants of Teddy's boyishness.

"Hi there," I managed to say. How long could I refrain from confessing that the breath in his body was the one thing keeping me alive? Ten minutes, ten seconds? "How you feeling?" I asked.

"Pretty bad. But I guess I must be better than I was. I heard I've been asleep for more than a week."

I sat in the rocker at his bedside. On his nightstand, a Bible was open to Psalms. "Yes," I said. "I'm happy that you're awake now. Everybody is."

"Including me," Teddy said, chuckling wryly. Then he turned serious. "There's so much still that I want to do in my life," he said. "So much that I want to do with you, so much that I want to experience and be a part of. But I'm also not afraid to die." Overnight, the young man had turned seasoned sage. "People are afraid to die, I think, because they're scared to find out that, in the end, they're just like everyone else. Everyone dies. In that, we are all exactly equal. Instead of pulling us together, that knowledge seems to rip us apart. It doesn't make any sense."

I moved over quickly to sit on the edge of the bed. "Oh, Teddy," I blurted out, "I love you so. I never want to be parted from you. Ever."

Teddy shifted over in the bed so I could lie down beside him. When he caught sight of my gloved hand, he gently took it in his hands, trying to detect broken bones without making me flinch.

"Don't you remember?" I asked. "On the morning you fell ill, my hand started to crack and blister from dragging a load of linens home. The lye drying out my skin set me up for it, I guess. After you fainted, I went to fetch water for you but had trouble getting the well cap off. That hurt it worse. It's better now. Ugly and tender, but better."

"Can I see it?" Teddy asked.

I carefully removed the glove and turned my hand so it was palm up. A thick red gash crossed it, like a primitive insignia. I wondered if it would ever heal.

"Lord." Teddy cradled my hand. "What you been putting on it?"

"Alder tree butter, like Old Lady Bronson said. It closed the wound and it don't hurt none unless I press on it hard."

"Then don't," Teddy begged. "Aloe should help with the scarring, so will letting air get to it. Why you wearing a glove?"

"'Cause I can't bear the sight of it."

"How 'bout tomorrow I look at it again for you and rub some aloe on it?"

I smiled without taking my hand from him. "You're the patient today, not the doctor."

"Helping somebody is the best medicine of all," Teddy said, and I couldn't disagree.

"Tell me about Joe Clarke and John Hurston," he

said. "What happened last night? Mama and Daddy stayed home with me, but Micah said he'd come by here afterward to give us a report. I was already asleep by the time he arrived, and this morning, my parents wouldn't say a word. No, that's not entirely true. Mama said, *It's not for you to worry about right now, Teddy.* Daddy said, *Listen to your mother.*"

I giggled, then said more seriously, "Well, truth is, it was awful, Teddy, especially for Mr. Clarke and Zora. Trying to defend Mr. Clarke against her father, Zora let slip that she believed Chester Cools was a zombie."

"Wait a second," Teddy said, his disbelief solidifying into mortification. "You're telling me that, last night, Zora told the whole town that she and Joe Clarke believe in zombies?"

"No, not Joe Clarke," I said, "but it came out that Mr. Clarke has known Chester thought he was a zombie for as long as he's run the town. Mr. Hurston had a way of making it sound like Mr. Clarke believed in zombies, on account of Joe thinking he needed to keep it a secret from everyone."

"You mean that, for eighteen years, Joe Clarke knew that Chester imagined he was a zombie?" Teddy was flabbergasted.

"Yes."

Teddy seemed to admire the willpower it must have taken to keep a secret like that.

"Besides that, Mr. Hurston practically disowned Zora, right there in front of everybody. Lucy Hurston's been real bad off. I'm going to the Hurstons' after I leave here."

Teddy was stunned. "Mr. Clarke keeps a person's confidence — for their own good, really — and now the town's decided to lose all confidence in Mr. Clarke."

"That's one way of looking at it," I concurred.

"Well, I can tell you how my parents see the character of the two mayoral candidates. Joe Clarke has been out here quite a bit to check on me and bring things. I don't think Mr. Hurston has been by once."

"That might be because Lucy Hurston is not doing well." I sighed. "Even before last night at the post office, Zora herself wasn't doing so hot. Right before you got sick, she and I went back to Mr. Cools's house, and I think that may have made everything worse."

"Why did you go back there?"

"Do you remember seeing a trunk when you were there with Doc Brazzle to get Mr. Cools's body?" I asked.

Teddy squinted through a persistent mental fog. "I can't remember for sure. Why?"

"Do you remember the day at school when Zora and Stella got into a fight?"

"That's a pretty hard thing to forget, Carrie."

"Well, once Zora got out of detention, that was the same day she and I went back to Chester Cools's place. I think being called a curse by Stella really got under her skin. I think she was determined to find proof that she wasn't. Cursed, I mean. I think she expected we'd find proof that Chester Cools was, in fact, a zombie."

"And did you find any?"

"Well, in a big fancy trunk, we found a camera and a lot of tintypes. One of them was of a lynched man." My stomach turned at the memory of the gruesome image. "Zora is convinced that the lynched man in the picture is Chester."

Teddy frowned. "I am, too," I admitted. "It looks so much like him. And it would explain the scars you saw while preparing his body for burial."

Teddy was quiet for a minute, thinking less about what he was going to say, I think, than about how he was going to say it. "Even if that picture is of Chester Cools," he said gently, "and I'm not saying it is or it isn't—people come *close* to death all the time and survive. Look at me. That's basically what I just did from the sounds of it. Chester could have done the same. Chester could have been cut down from that tree. He could have been spared."

I picked up the Bible and fingered it nervously.

"What is it, Carrie? There's something else you're not saying. I can tell."

"On those tintypes," I began. "Ink, but not ink. Something black and gooey, feeding on the images, the people. Some of it got on Zora's hand. She told me that, since that day, she feels different, cold and filled with dread."

"Did any of it get on you?" Teddy asked.

"No."

"Sounds more to me like Zora is coming down with something," he said, sounding practical, like a doctor, blaming the natural instead of the supernatural world. "And that it just happened to hit her on that day. Coincidence, Carrie."

I said nothing.

"I hope it's not whatever I've had," Teddy added with false cheer.

"I hope not," I said, to placate him and, maybe, myself. "Would you like me to read aloud to you?"

I asked, indicating the Bible, changing the subject.

"That would be nice."

Before I had settled on a passage, let alone read a single word, Teddy's eyes shuttered closed. I was thankful beyond words that Teddy Baker had come through the flames of his illness intact. I hoped and prayed that Zora and Eatonville could survive their crucibles, too.

CHAPTER TWENTY-ONE

A long the road, out front the Hurston house, a fleet of automobiles, including John Hurston's beautiful chariot, stood suspended like a petrified parade.

I opened and closed the gate and headed for the house. On the front porch, East was offering Sarah preemptive congratulations. "You're going to be the daughter of the mayor! It'll probably be a first for a colored girl, a first! Y'all Hurstons are like royalty."

Under the weight of flattery, Sarah's modesty crumbled. "You think so?" she asked.

Zora stepped out onto the porch. "Well, it is a title you'd share with me," she said. Zora's eyes were puffy. She had been crying. "Hi, Carrie."

"Hey," I responded. "Where did all the horse-lesses come from?"

"That gray one—" East pointed to a storm cloud of a Ford. "That's mine and brand spanking new!"

"It's real nice," I said politely.

Zora rolled her eyes. "They all are nice," she said, "even my father's, which he made sure the whole town got a look at yesterday. But they're just cars. It's the people who rode up in them from Alabama and Georgia to kiss my father's behind that are questionable."

"Given how tender you've been with Mama, and given how hard last night must have been on you, I'm gonna act like I didn't hear that, Zora," Sarah chided.

"Your little sister ain't very proud of your pappy," East butted in. "She ain't very respectful of him either, and she certainly isn't grateful. I don't think she appreciates that being the colored children of a colored mayor is something to shout from the treetops!"

Zora lobbed a long contemptuous look at East. Sarah blushed. "Oh, East," she managed. "Zora's more like Daddy than anyone else in this house. That's why she's so full of pride." Sarah juggled her loyalties. "Ain't that the truth, Zora?"

Rather than answer the question, Zora had questions to turn on East. "Do you really want to take care of my sister?" she asked him. "Or do you want my father's name to take care of *you*?"

"Zora!" Sarah admonished, horrified. "Apologize! Now! On account of your presumptuousness! Apologize!"

East took Sarah's outrage as confirmation that she and he were allies. He took one of Sarah's hands and caressed it, as if offering her protection from Zora.

Zora saw through East's charade and dug in. "No. Not to him."

In the next moment, Zora seemed to look into the future and catch a glimpse of her sister's possible future with East. "I am sorry," Zora said with genuine feeling, "for you, Sarah. I really am."

The dismal future Zora seemed to be intimating for her sent Sarah spiraling into fragile, speechless uncertainty.

"I need to get away from here," Zora said to no one in particular. "Carrie, you mind going for a walk with me?"

"Not at all," I answered.

Out of the corner of my eye, I saw Sarah surreptitiously remove her hand from East's.

"Why don't you come with us, Sarah?" I suggested, hoping against hope she'd take the lifeline. "The house is full of people. Somebody can look after your mother for a few minutes."

Sarah shut down her feelings. "No. I'm fine," she said, straightening. "Mama needs me."

Nothing was fine.

Zora and I headed north on the road. I peeked in the windows of all the automobiles as we passed them. Silver gears and knobs, like the inner workings of a clock, protruded from the dashboards. I was reminded of Mr. Cools's camera.

"I told Teddy about us going back to Mr. Cools's cabin," I said. "And about what we found there."

"How is Teddy?" Zora asked, ignoring most of what I had just said.

"Well, mostly he sounds like himself, but he definitely doesn't look like himself. He's still awfully thin. I expect he'll improve. I hope so."

"He will," Zora reassured me. "Teddy getting better is the best news we've had in weeks."

"It certainly is," I seconded. We walked in silence for a while, but Zora couldn't keep her feelings inside for long.

"I can't understand it!" she blurted out. "Sarah's been acting like she'd happily dive into a gator swamp for a chance at a wedding ring."

"Looks like she fell in love," I said.

"More like she slipped and fell off a cliff!"

"We walking anywhere in particular, Zora? Someplace you had in mind?"

"Well," she answered sulkily, "I'm itching to go talk to Joe Clarke, but I don't imagine Mr. Clarke wants to talk to anyone named Hurston ever again."

"You were trying to help when you spoke your piece yesterday. He knows that."

"Why didn't Joe tell us what he knew about Chester the day we were all at the cemetery? He should have. If he had," Zora said, "I might not have made such a fool of myself yesterday and, more importantly, wouldn't have made things that much easier for my father. . . .

"The Terrace Side lynching and Chester's grave robbery put a knife in the heart of this town. I helped to turn it." She was beside herself with shame.

"Maybe the sooner I leave Eatonville, the better off I'll be, the better off Eatonville will be. Maybe I *am* a curse."

Zora's self-pity made me boil over. "Seriously, Zora? Since when did you start listening to the likes of Stella Brazzle?"

Zora had no answer for that.

"And I'm beginning to think," I snapped, "that you're as bad as your father, who thinks everything is about him! Well, it's not. You are not your father and you are not a curse and you are not responsible for every single thing that happens in Eatonville! Stop feeling sorry for yourself and just be a better you."

Zora looked at me in open-mouthed surprise.

I immediately regretted my outburst. But after a moment, she simply said, "You're right."

Then we walked to Joe Clarke's, each having stunned the other into silence.

CHAPTER TWENTY-TWO

Mr. Clarke's porch was empty. The store was, too, but we could hear voices coming from the back of the store, where Mr. Clarke had an office. We followed the voices and Zora knocked on the door. The voices fell silent and Old Lady Bronson opened the door. Joe Clarke was the only other person in the office. He was sitting behind his desk.

"What you two doing here?" the old woman asked, but not in any way unfriendly. "Still trying to thwart democracy?" she added with a wink.

"Um, no," I answered bashfully.

"I came here to apologize to Joe," Zora said, her

eyes on Mr. Clarke. Old Lady Bronson stepped aside so the two friends could see each other. "I should have kept my mouth shut during the debate," Zora continued. "Things were already bad and I made them worse. I'm sorry, Mr. Clarke. So sorry."

Old Lady Bronson heaved a sympathetic sigh. Mr. Clarke stood, went around to the front of his large, smooth desk, and sat on its edge. "You were the only one who came to my defense," he said. Far from angry, Joe Clarke was touched. "This town has taken a lot from me. It's also given me much more than my share. One of the best things Eatonville ever gave me, Zora, was you."

Zora relaxed with relief and gratitude. "I can't believe the fool I've been," she said, regret still reddening her eyes. "Today, I've finally woken up to the fact that every time something really bad has happened in Eatonville, the culprit hasn't been a monster, a ghost, or a curse." She paused. "It was a white man passing through here that murdered Ivory. It was a white man who stabbed Mr. Polk in the hopes of stealing his land. It was a mob of white men that lynched Terrace Side. And it looks likely that white folks, some of these so-called resurrection men, had a hand in the fate of Mr. Cools, too."

168

Mr. Clarke was quiet, just listening.

"Whatever made Mr. Cools think he was a zombie?" Zora asked. "Did he ever tell you?"

Mr. Clarke gave a sad, toothless smile: "Eighteen years ago, when I was a young man, this store was still just a shell. Afternoons, Chester lent me a hand hammering beams. I was grateful. The lumber to build my store cost so much, I ain't have three red cents for an actual hire. I was also lonely. Evenings, we'd talk.

"One night after our work was finished, we sat here, me drinking moonshine; Chester never touched the stuff. That night, he said he had blood on his mind. I figured he meant revenge and was gonna tell me how his mama or wife or child had been sold away from him on an auction block. But that wasn't what he was talking about. Not at all.

"Next thing, Chester lifted his pants leg, pulled a jack knife from his boot, and unfolded the blade. Before I knew what he was about, he slashed his own forearm. I jumped clear outta my chair. Chester bled normal at first—red, like you and me—but then the blood turned black, like ink. Chester made sure I got a good look at that strange blood before he staunched the bleeding with a rag. I was sure the moonshine had snatched or scrambled my mind. Then Chester began to tell me a story, a goddamned wretched story."

An icy chill gripped my chest, remembering the blotch from my nightmare. Zora looked down at her hands, I think remembering the blackness from the photograph that had bled onto her skin.

Mr. Clarke rubbed his eyes and loosened from his brain a ghastly tale he would prefer not to have heard. He said, "When he was a boy, Chester lived in Atlanta. On the outskirts of Atlanta at that time, there was a doctor named Sumner. This Dr. Sumner ain't own any slaves outright. Strange, especially for such a wealthy man. What he had, instead, was a distillery. From miles around, folks came to buy Sumner's whiskey.

"To help him with his operation, he rented young boy slaves, those who weren't much use to their masters yet, like Chester was then. The slave owners thought they had quite a deal. Sumner was readying these boys for the real work they'd be expected to do someday. The slaves themselves started calling the doctor by a different name: the Summoner. He called children away from the world of the living to another, one consumed by death.

"Turns out, the distillery was not the only piece of the operation. No one outside was aware that the doctor was also doing other . . . work. Sumner had become fascinated with photography, with its ability to capture a likeness, a moment in time, and thus preserve it forever. He had also become obsessed with the idea of reanimation: bringing the dead back to life." Joe paused to let that sink in for a moment. Zora was riveted; I was repulsed.

"His experiments demanded corpses," Joe continued. "So Chester, like most of the smallest and youngest boys, began his horrible apprenticeship by first learning how to pick locks. Eventually the doctor did away with lock picking altogether; he had cut a set of skeleton keys that could open a range of deadlocks used on crypts and cemetery gates across Georgia. Some of that same whiskey the Summoner was known for was used to preserve stolen corpses in big barrels that lined the cellar. The whiskey masked the stench of death.

"When the Summoner began building a camera, the boys were more afraid of it than the pickled bodies. With its one big gaping eye, it seemed alive. The Summoner believed that the camera held the secret to unlocking the mystery of death itself, which further terrified the boys."

"During the war and after," Old Lady Bronson

added, "I remember spiritualist photographers popping up everywhere. They made fortunes selling folks supposed portraits of their dead loved ones from the other side, claiming that the camera could see what the naked eye couldn't: spirits. This Summoner was a little different. He was trying to instill spirit himself. He fancied himself a god."

Joe Clarke nodded and went on. "When Chester outgrew his use to the Summoner, he was replaced by someone younger and smaller. Chester went back to being a house slave. But the passing years eventually brought the war, and many slaves escaped and fled to join the Union's campaign: women and girls to be wartime domestics, tending to laundry and preparing gruel, men and boys to be soldiers. On his own way to join the fight for freedom, Chester was caught by a group of Confederate soldiers and lynched. "

Zora gasped. I trembled.

"And that's when Chester was reunited with the Summoner," said Joe Clarke. "The Summoner had heard that Chester was going to be lynched and arrived to photograph Chester while he was still hanging from the tree. Then he cut Chester down, claimed the body, which nobody else wanted, and laid it on a cooling board in his cellar.

"There, Chester began to breathe again. He was alive. The Summoner, convinced that he had resurrected Chester, tended to Chester's wounds, set his bones, and nursed him back to health, which took months. Chester was to be the Summoner's trophy, proof that his experiment had finally worked: that his camera could bring a man back to life. It was the tale the Summoner told Chester again and again —and anyone else who would listen. And why wouldn't Chester, who remembered the noose tightening around his neck, the rope cutting into his throat from the weight of his own body, believe him?"

I shivered. We had been right. Chester *was* the lynched man in the picture.

After a moment, Zora asked, "Whatever happened to the Summoner?"

"Buildings in Atlanta that had not been outright destroyed by cannon fire in the war were greatly compromised by Sherman," Joe said. "Chester told me that the Summoner was killed in the collapse of his own place. Chester even buried the doctor himself."

I could almost see the wheels in Zora's mind turning and turning. "In a trunk back at Chester's," she cried, "we found a camera, and we found tintypes, too! I think it must be the Summoner's camera!

Why else would it be there in Chester's house? And we saw the stuff you saw Chester bleed, Mr. Clarke. It got on my hand! That stuff is real. It got on my hand from one of the pictures, one of those awful pictures!"

"God, Chester had that man's camera? I wish I'd known." Shame shook Mr. Clarke to the core. "I could have changed Chester's mind."

"That wasn't your burden, Joe," Old Lady Bronson consoled. "Do you actually think you could have changed Chester's mind after all these years?"

A faithfulness to mystery, to strange unknowable symmetries, vibrated Zora. "Chester Cools really was a zombie," she said.

Joe Clarke scowled. "Have you been listening to a single thing we've been saying, Zora?"

"Yes, and it sounded a lot to me like Chester was lynched, then brought back to life by this Summoner and his evil camera, and that he had black blood flowing through his veins as proof, proof you saw yourself."

Mr. Clarke looked at Zora with a certainty that pained him. "Chester Cools was not a zombie. He survived that lynching, accidentally cut down before he was completely dead. The Summoner lied to Chester, maybe he even lied to himself. He did not resurrect Chester. A lynching got Chester in the end, just not his own and not in the way you'd think. The horror of what happened to Terrace Side is what killed Chester. Like it was happening all over again.

"I didn't see it that day on the porch when Chester lost his wits, but I see it now." Joe Clarke looked sadder than I'd ever seen.

A horrible thought came to me. I believed Mr. Clarke and Old Lady Bronson that Chester Cools had survived his own lynching, but is merely surviving the same as living? I think Chester Cools understood perfectly what he had become: a zombie, which by another name meant the victim of trauma who'd never really healed.

One look at Zora, and I could see that she had yet to be convinced. Recognizing this, Old Lady Bronson took Zora's hand and said, "Come back to my place with me, Zora. I've got a book for you. That book might have enough truth in it for you, dear girl, even for you."

CHAPTER TWENTY-THREE

The next time I visited Teddy, he already had company. Zora sat in his desk chair with a book open in her lap while Teddy occupied the nook at his bedside; from opposite sides of the room, the two faced off. I felt like a referee as soon as I plunked down on the bed.

Teddy shifted in his chair, into the sunlight. His sunken chest had a bowl curve, beautiful and frail. He asked Zora, "Have you told Carrie any of what you just told me?"

"No," she answered. "I thought I'd bring it to you first since you're the scientist."

"Bring what?" I inquired.

"This." She held up the book. "It's what Old Lady Bronson wanted to show me."

I squinted at the spine. The gold leaf script had too many curves and curlicues for me to make out the words.

"It's called *The Transformation Philosophorum*," she said. "It's about alchemy."

"*Alka*-what?"

"Alchemy," Teddy said, "the process of changing metals into gold. Nowadays folks call it hoodoo chemistry, on account of the fact that no one has ever managed to make it work."

"A lot of folks think a good deal of science is hoodoo," Zora objected. "Some of the folks my father preaches to don't trust a word that comes out of any book other than the Bible. Those folks are afraid of hoodoo *and* of science because those might offer more sensible explanations for things they don't or can't understand. But what makes turning ordinary metal into gold any less possible than turning water into wine? Ever see anybody make that work? Now, take this stuff that got on me from the pictures in Mr. Cools's trunk," Zora continued. "I believe it's the exact same stuff that Mr. Clarke saw bleeding from

Chester's arm. And this book here tells me it's called *nigredo*. Why shouldn't I believe this book just as much as I'm told to believe the Bible?"

Zora stood, stomped across Teddy's room with the tome, and dropped it in his lap. "Here," she said. "I'm open-minded, Mr. Science. Are you? Read."

"From the beginning?"

"Yes," Zora commanded.

Teddy read:

"The science of alchemy consists of three independent operations. The colors of these operations represent and embody the rainbow of transformative capabilities possible for the trained alchemist to achieve. The pigments of the subterranean world are *nigredo*, the black; *albedo*, the white; and *rubedo*, the red. *Nigredo* is of particular interest to the alchemist set on perfecting the act of creation or resurrection.

The properties of *nigredo* belong to the chemical process of *mortifactio*, the program of death. Birth, new life, cannot emerge without first undergoing *mortifactio*. The sleep of death, the darkness of death, is the only habitat, the

only process, truly suitable for the awaken-
ing of a new life. It is said that God separated
darkness from light. *Nigredo* is the descendent
of the original darkness, god-matter. If the
maker, the God, if you will, is good, then the
nigredo is good, a balm. If the maker is evil, then
the *nigredo* is the water of evil. The embodi-
ment of the nothing that is everything, *nigredo*
can never be destroyed."

My skin crawled. The idea that mere mortals could
have at their fingertips the primordial and unendingly
flexible source of life and the ability to control it,
frightened me. People already had free will. People
had already created versions of Heaven and Hell right
here on Earth. Wasn't that more than enough?

Teddy stopped reading but didn't lift his eyes
from the page. Something in these strange words had
gotten to him. Recognition came over his face. He
might have lacked the imagination that brilliantly
colored Zora's world, but Teddy's commonsense
worldview was far from impoverished. "The stuff you
got on your hand, Zora," he said thoughtfully. "You
know what it sounds like to me?"

"*Nigredo,*" Zora offered stubbornly.

"Black mercury," he said, ignoring her sass.

Zora was suddenly all ears. *Black mercury* sounded as tantalizing as *nigredo*.

"I can't believe I'm just remembering this now," Teddy said. "The photographer who came to our house to take Micah and Daisy's wedding portrait—I asked him about the chemical process used to transfer images, and he said that he used black mercury. It's an element, a heavy metal. It doesn't evaporate like water. The dark trunk probably provided ideal conditions for preserving the chemical. It would make sense that traces of it would still be on the tintypes."

"Even after all these years?" Zora did not sound convinced by Teddy's scientific explanation.

"Is black mercury dangerous?" I worried.

"I wouldn't drink the stuff if that's what you're asking," Teddy said. "But I don't really know. Do you suppose all that stuff and the trunk are still at Chester's place?" he asked us.

"I don't know," Zora replied absently. She was no longer really talking to us. Her mind, her thoughts, were somewhere else altogether, I could tell. "I wonder," she murmured, then quietly repeated a line from

The Transformation Rosarium: "If the maker is good, then the *nigredo* is good."

Teddy, dear Teddy, understood immediately what was going on. "Zora," he said very gently, "even if you . . . managed to take a picture of your mother . . . even if that somehow worked . . . or did whatever you think it would do . . . what then?"

My realization of just how deep Zora's desperation went didn't come to me as quickly as it had to Teddy, but it still hit me like a brick. What Zora seemed willing to latch on to to keep from drowning in her ocean of grief took my breath away.

Zora didn't answer Teddy, and neither I nor Teddy could come up with anything more to say. In that moment, I suspect we both told ourselves that the entire conversation had been no more than a medicinal measure for our friend.

CHAPTER TWENTY-FOUR

In the entirety of the South, white people had wiped out black people's right to vote using tests, taxes, and threats. For many reasons then, Eatonville's mayoral election of 1905 was a rare event in the history and life of these United States. We were exercising our power to mount a free and fair election. Enfranchised colored folks decided on the date, time, and place we would choose a man to lead us. A lot of skin was in the game. Since all of it was brown, white folks didn't seem to care very much.

The voting began at the post office on Saturday at sunrise. By three, everyone eligible had cast a ballot.

Around four, Mama and I, along with the rest of the town and the candidates, returned to the post office to hear the results.

In front of his automobile's large metal grille, John Hurston appeared to still be speechifying, a large group orbiting him like bees around sugar. In the vehicle's back seat, Lucy Hurston languished. Seated beside her was an old woman I recognized as Lucy's mother, Zora's grandmother.

On the lawn, Joe Clarke chatted more casually with a small group of supporters, many of whom lived in Lake Catherine and Blue Bay and so were not eligible to vote. Bo Wilson plucked away at a tune on the banjo as I sat with Zora, fretting, on the post office steps.

"Did you see my grandmother over there?" Zora asked.

"Yes. When did she get here?"

"Last night. Just in time for this," she spat. "I think Grandma Potts is more alarmed by my father's success than she is my mother's illness."

The Alabama woman had never thought John Hurston was good enough for her daughter. As his success grew, her visits diminished, until she stopped visiting altogether. Seeing as this visit coincided with her son-in-law's possible coronation as mayor of a town, Mrs. Potts must have thought she couldn't delay seeing her daughter another day, another hour. The realization made my stomach drop.

Mr. Johnson emerged from the post office holding a piece of paper, and everyone instantly shushed and froze. Mr. Hurston and Joe Clarke approached the steps of the porch.

Mr. Johnson stepped down the stairs and shook John Hurston's hand. Cheers and praise erupted. "Congratulations, John," Mr. Johnson shouted over the noise of the crowd. "You have been duly elected the next mayor of Eatonville, Florida."

Mr. Hurston touched his heart and gazed heavenward in gratitude. Joe Clarke extended his hand to Mr. Hurston. Mr. Hurston took it but was already gliding away toward his horseless, acting like Mr. Clarke was nothing more than another nameless, faceless fan. Mrs. Potts, looking fussed, had opened the door of the vehicle to help her daughter get out and go stand beside her victorious husband. East, seeing an opportunity, leaped out of the throng to come to their aid.

Lucy Hurston's scalp sagged beneath thin, threadlike hair. Her eyes looked grotesquely large on her thin, gray face. John Hurston swept her up and draped an arm over her shoulders, as though she were the prize and he her maker. Sick as she was, Lucy Hurston stood strong under the weight of her husband's pride, just as proud and pleased herself. Together, she and John had come a long way. Together, they did not have much further to go.

CHAPTER TWENTY-FIVE

Three months into Mayor John Hurston's six-year term, Lucy took to her bed. At John Hurston's insistence, both Old Lady Bronson and Doc Brazzle came to examine her together. After the joint examination, the sage and the physician appeared before the family, huddled and waiting in the front room.

"She doesn't have long," Doc Brazzle said, stating the shared verdict.

John Hurston left for Lucy's bedroom first. Bob, Sarah, Everett, and Zora followed, sobbing. I rose to accompany them, but Old Lady Bronson held me back. "Come help me," she said, and led me into the kitchen.

There, Old Lady Bronson pointed to the clock over the cupboard. I immediately understood the task at hand and the comprehension caused my chest to heave. According to superstition, the way to honor the sum of a life was to stop and mark the time before a soul departed this world for the next. If the clocks were not halted, in time, the superstition foretold, the flow of bad luck for anyone present at the death would never cease. Such were the pagan precautions that had to be taken, even in a minister's home, to account for mysteries outside of Christ.

I dragged over a chair, stood on it, and took the metal timepiece down. It read quarter past eight. Old Lady Bronson opened the back, reached in, removed a small rusted weight from the chain, and dropped the modest pendulum into one of her large apron pockets. I returned the clock to the wall.

Another clock sat on the buffet in the dining room, where Mrs. Potts cried, hunched over the table. When she registered what we were doing, her nostrils flared.

"Stop it," she commanded, "right now! It's not time! She has more time!" John Hurston stepped into the room to see what the fuss was about. A thick string of snot hovered above her lip. Mrs. Potts swatted at it, the way you might swat at a fly or a gnat, which just spread the slimy smear to her cheek. John Hurston pulled a white handkerchief from his pocket. Wordlessly he wiped her nose and face, like he would have a child's. It was the kindest thing I had ever seen him do. He folded the handkerchief and placed it in his mother-in-law's trembling hand. "I'm going to the solarium for a few minutes," he said. "I need to be alone. Leave Old Lady Bronson to her tasks before it's too late."

The agony of Mrs. Potts's sorrow was like a punch to the gut, and she doubled over. "Too late," she moaned at her son-in-law's back. "Too late . . ."

Old Lady Bronson opened the clock, pulled the minute hand from the face, and slipped it into her apron pocket, where she had stowed the other time bits. Old Lady Bronson stopped time with the same expert precision she used to birth babies and reel in fish, to wring chicken necks and reset bones. I was struck by how that single pair of hands could tear things asunder as easily as they could stitch them together, keep folks alive.

Lucy Hurston's bedroom held the last working timepiece.

When we stepped in, the first thing we saw was Sarah, Bob, and Everett standing in a cluster by their mother's bedside, soldiers mourning a fallen general. Then we registered Zora's presence in the room. She stood at the foot of Lucy's bed, apart from her siblings, refusing to surrender. My heart sank and horror washed over me. Was I imagining this, or had Zora lost her mind? Old Lady Bronson provided the answer.

"Lord, child," she scolded Zora. "Take that thing down! Carrie, help Zora get that thing out of sight, before her daddy sees. Help her, now!"

At the foot of her mother's deathbed, Zora was in the process of setting up an old camera on a wooden chair and focusing its lens on Lucy. It put me in mind of a cannon. It was the camera from Chester Cools's cabin, the Summoner's camera. Zora must have gone back and retrieved it. How she managed it on her own, I didn't know.

"I told Zora not to!" Bob spat, tears streaming down his face. "But she won't listen." He stormed out of the room, more boy than man. Sarah hugged

Everett to her, hiding his face from the scene.

I stepped over to Zora and put a hand on her arm. "How?" I managed to squeak before faltering.

"After I read about *nigredo*," she said to me, her eyes shining with hope, "I went back to Mr. Cools's place for the camera. I dragged it clear across Eatonville in an old wagon. The strangest part, Carrie, is that I didn't run into a single soul. It was as if my path had been cleared of obstacles, like I was meant to have this camera. Once I got it here to the house, I hid it under Mama's bed, knowing that, one day soon, I would have need of it."

"Mr. Cools had a miserable life," I reminded her. "Maybe the Summoner *did* bring him back to life. Maybe Chester *was* a zombie. Do you think he liked it? Do you think that's how he wanted to live? Do you think that's what your mother would want? Is that really what you would want for her?"

"If there is any chance that I could keep Mama here on this earth for a day, a week, a month longer, I have to try. I couldn't live with myself if I didn't at least try," she said.

Before my eyes, my oldest friend had turned into an unfathomable mystery. "No matter," I prodded, "if you kill some part of your soul and hers in the process?"

"Yes."

"I can't let that happen," I said, and tugged at the chair. The heavy machine wobbled, and that's when John Hurston detonated into the room. He was followed by Bob, Doc Brazzle, and Mrs. Potts.

John Hurston gaped at the camera in disbelief. "What's this?" he snarled, then glared at Zora. "What in God's name are you doing?"

Lucy Hurston stirred in her bed, fluttered ever so slightly, silently.

Zora returned all of her focus to the camera and her mother, ignoring her father, ignoring me and Old Lady Bronson.

John Hurston had had enough. He kicked the chair, which sent it sliding into the dresser. Zora lunged to keep the camera from crashing to the floor. "I just want a picture of Mama," she cried. "Just one! Please, Daddy! Please! It might save her!"

But John Hurston took one giant step toward Zora and thwacked her on the side of her head. Zora fell to the floor, and the camera flew from her hands. Eatonville's new mayor lifted a foot and, giving Zora a death stare, stomped on the camera until we could hear the grit of shattered glass grinding the floorboards. The only respite was that he wasn't thrashing Zora.

"This is not how we're going to remember my wife!" John Hurston raged.

Then, bowed by his sorrow and exhausted by his violent anguish, he collapsed amid the ruins of the machine and wept. He must have cut himself on a shard of glass, because when he put his hand to his face, he smeared his cheek with blood.

Zora got up from the floor. She stepped over her father's spiritual remains, stepped past the defeated remains of her family, and climbed into bed beside her mother. She gently pressed her lips to Lucy's face, stroked her hair, and listened to her mother breathe her last breath. In it, I think, Zora heard the resounding sound of a door closing, the first of many that would slam shut over the course of her life.

CHAPTER TWENTY-SIX

To prepare Lucy for the wake and funeral, Old Lady Bronson and Mrs. Potts dabbed her face for hours with cloths soaked in soda water to keep the death look at bay. A scarf tied around her head and under her chin kept her lips from parting, and nickels weighted her eyelids. A cold lodger in her wedding dress, Lucy Hurston looked more like a child bride than a corpse.

Mourners arrived with sunflowers, pennyroyal, and wild sweet william. Bloom-filled vases, glasses, and porcelain bowls lined the path from the Hurston front gate to the house, and the house itself swam with scent. Black curtains hung in the living room and the solarium. Gardenia-scented columns stood at each end of the coffin, which, at ninety dollars, was the most expensive any of us had ever heard of. John Hurston had bought it in Daytona. It was made of mahogany, lined with red velvet, and decked out with solid silver bolts. Lucy Hurston's final resting place was a far cry from that toothpick box Chester Cools had been buried in.

Eatonville hosted the funeral at Hurston's church, New Hope Macedonia, but Mrs. Potts insisted that Lucy be buried in the Potts family plot in Alabama, a whole state away, laid to final rest beside her sister and infant nephew. To everyone's surprise, John Hurston easily agreed. The theft of Chester Cools's body still cast a shadow over Eatonville, and the widower couldn't stomach the risk of having his wife buried at Sand Grounds and suffer the same fate.

Just as they had for the mayoral election, many of John Hurston's out-of-town followers traveled to Eatonville to pay their respects. The same chairs that had been used for the debate were now set up on the lawn outside of the church. Only there weren't enough. Lots of men, women, and children had to stand.

The minister who had baptized Lucy, in the

church where John Hurston had first spotted her as a girl, presided. His name was Roscoe Locke. "The first time I ever beheld Lucy Potts," he recalled, "she was a shut-eyed infant rooting for her mama's breast. 'Fore long, she was a stout-legged, milk-bellied toddler; then, a knee-scraped wiry girl; and finally, a beautiful woman. Again now and forevermore, in God's arms she's that little baby, unable to open her eyes because God's glory is star-bright. His embrace is soft and steady, and the milk of His salvation is warm and sweet and good. We'll miss dear Lucy, but our hearts are glad 'cause she lives now in God's arms and her spirit can reach high and wide enough to do the heavens a few favors, like she done down here for all of us.

"She'll brighten up that dull ol' boulder, the moon, like she brightened up our lives here on this earth. She'll open up a window and door on that moon so it can catch, each and every day, a little more sun, a little more warmth. In turn, that glow will stream down on us every night and in every dark moment of our lives." Reverend Locke looked down on Lucy in her rest, touched Lucy's folded hands, and bowed his head in silent prayer for a few moments. Then he brought the coffin lid down over Lucy, slowly, surely, finally.

Zora wailed. Her anguish rattled my teeth. Mama

tucked her head into my shoulder and poured hot tears on my neck. I felt tired and small and so sad. The grief in the church hammered like a storm that was a song and a song that was a storm.

When the family returned from the burial in Alabama, my mother and I went by the Hurstons' to see how we could help. John Hurston had gone out for a drive. Curled up like a newborn in the window seat, Everett slept while Bob packed for his return to Orlando, and Zora took refuge in Lucy's feather bed, soaking up her mama's scent. Sarah was puttering around the kitchen, moving platters and silverware that had been used at the repast without putting any one thing away. All of the glassware and bowls that held the funeral bouquets had been collected, but dried petals and blackened leaves littered the floor. Mama guided Sarah over to the kitchen table, sat her down, and began sorting out the special occasion items from the everyday wares. Out back, on the steps, I found two full sacks of laundry.

"Anything you want done with those things on the back porch?" I asked.

"It's dirty laundry. Daddy's and East's," Sarah said, her voice dry, empty.

East? His laundry? They weren't even engaged, let alone married, and he had left his soiled things at a house in mourning? If that didn't disqualify him as a suitor, I wasn't sure what would.

"I'll see to it," I answered, feeling even worse for Sarah. "I see y'all got a laundry barrel out back now, not too far from the old chicken coop," I said. "I'll sort it out there."

"I'll get the fire going and boil the water," Sarah said. "I don't want you to get that hand wet."

I smiled, thankful to see Sarah was still there, under her grief.

While the water was readied, I decided to sweep the flowers that had been colorful and velvety with life but were now withered to crepey gray crumbs.

Though my hand ached, I cleaned up the front porch, the foyer, the front room, and the solarium. When I was done with that, I grabbed the sack I assumed to be East's because it was smaller and dragged it to the makeshift washing station to sort. The fire was blazing now, the water in the barrel boiling. Mama came out with a bar of store-bought soap and dropped it into the water. We stood together in silence for a moment, watching the fragrant steam rise.

"That was Lucy. Always making things nice."

Mama paused in homage to her friend, then said, "When you think they done soaking long enough, come get me. I'll come out and scrub 'em while you help Sarah straighten out the kitchen. Need to keep that hand of yours dry."

"All right." I emptied the sack onto a tarp. Two shirts, two pairs of slacks, an undershirt, a few pairs of drawers, and some holey socks tumbled out. East's bowler fell out last, a cross between an omen and a punctuation mark. I shook out his garments and threw them into the barrel, out of sight, one at a time. There were only socks and the hat and a single pair of trousers left on the ground. When I picked up the last pair of trousers, I could feel that there was something in the pocket. I reached into the pocket with my ungloved hand. A moment later, I was staring at a long silver nail. The initials BE were engraved on its large, flat head. Bertram Edges had smithed this nail. He had smithed this nail for one purpose: to seal Chester Cools's coffin. I nearly lost my footing.

I gripped the thing tightly, ran around the front of the house to avoid Mama and Sarah, and bolted into Lucy's bedroom to wake Zora. The last time I had been in this room, I watched a father crush his youngest daughter's dream of snatching her mother from death. I faltered for a moment. Now I was about to crush the elder daughter's hopes for a happy future.

"Zora." I touched her arm firmly. Zora's eyes remained closed. "Wake up!" I demanded. "It's important!"

Zora turned onto her back and opened her eyes. "What is it?" she asked groggily.

I held out the nail. "I discovered this in East's pocket."

A moment passed before Zora registered what was in my hand. "It's a nail," she said flatly.

"Not just any nail," I said bitterly.

Zora frowned, took the nail from me, and examined it. She sat up, suddenly wide awake. "My God!" she exclaimed. "*BE.* Bertram Edges. Mr. Edges made this." She stared at the nail, putting the pieces together. She looked up at me. "This was in East's pocket?" she asked.

I nodded.

"It's like he kept this as a trophy," she said. "A trophy! What kind of person does that? What kind?"

"The grave-robbing kind," I said, putting it bluntly.

That nail suddenly represented for us everything that had happened in Eatonville in the last couple of months, everything that had come hammering down on us. The manhunt and the lynching; Chester Cools going crazy, then dying; the grave robbery; Teddy's illness; the election; Lucy Hurston's passing. Nails are meant to keep pictures on the wall, hold furniture together, and keep houses standing. This nail had helped rip our town apart.

"We have to tell Sarah!"

While I knew she was right, I wished more than anything right then that we could make the nail disappear, that we could erase what it undoubtedly signified.

"She's in the kitchen with my mother."

Zora took a deep breath and headed to the heart of the house, angry at the discovery of the nail but terrified, I know, by what she had to do. She entered the kitchen with me at her heels. "You come to say goodbye to your big brother?" Bob asked Zora. "East here is gonna take me to the station."

East stood near the back door, looking smugger than he had right to be, surrounded as he was by children who'd just lost their mother. As long as East was fine, everything was fine; it mattered very little to him that the worlds of the people around him had burned. "Your mama tells me you started my laundry," East said to me. "Thank you."

"You won't be thanking anyone in a minute," Zora said.

Sarah stirred in her chair. "Zora, what are you talking about?"

Zora held out the nail on the platter of her palm and swiveled so everyone could see. "Carrie found this in East's pocket."

East maintained his composure while puzzled confusion came over my mother. What was all the fuss over an ordinary nail in the pocket of a young man?

Bob grimaced. He had been through enough already and had no patience for some new hurtful craziness from Zora. Sarah sat blankly at the table. "Zora, what's this all about?" Bob snapped. "East needs to get me to the station."

Piqued, Zora said, "Before you leave, why don't East tell us where he got this nail?"

"I do apologize for not emptying my pockets 'fore I dropped off my things." There was an edge to his voice that blunted his apology. "I'm always fixing one thing or another, mainly to do with my business. I must have been hammering something, had more nails than I needed in my pocket, and just forgot it was there."

"You didn't fix anything with that nail!" I hissed, beside myself with his lies. "This nail is proof you helped rob Chester Cools from his grave!"

The air in the room had turned into water. Almost everyone was drowning in disbelief.

Zora pointed at East with righteous certainty. "This silver nail was smithed special by Bertram Edges for Mr. Cools's coffin. We can go to Mr. Edges's workshop this minute and ask him, but we don't have to, do we, East? Why would you have this if you didn't have something to do with the grave robbery?"

"Let's calm down," Bob urged, still hoping his sister and I were out of our minds but sounding less dismissive. "There must be an explanation for this strange coincidence, right, East? And you should have the chance to explain."

"Yes," Sarah said, trying to appear calm and composed. She struggled to say something further, but her chest was rising and falling rapidly, and she could barely catch her breath. Finally, she managed, "Please, I need you to explain." East's eyes grew soft, but strangely so, like an opaque rind of fat on a cut of meat.

"I love you, Sarah," he began. "I have since the moment I laid eyes on you at your father's church the day of the wedding. I didn't know that fella who tied the knot. I fibbed and said I did, but I was there for no other reason than to get a peek at Eatonville's finest. And I did. I saw you. I want to marry you, darlin'. I do. More than anything in this world, I want to marry you."

As Sarah listened, her breath stabilized and her hands stopped shaking. It seemed like something true and abiding steadied her. I couldn't tell if it was disgust or true love. "So how'd you get that nail?" she asked. "You were going to explain that."

"Like I said, I'm set on marrying you, but I'm not from means. And I'd have to work a long, long time carrying folks all around the state before I earn enough money for a fine house like this. I'm saving, though, pinching every penny, and I'm working hard. One day I reckon, with your help, I'll become a big man like your daddy. With God's help, hopefully here in Eatonville, I'll become a prosperous man.

"I'm strong and I ain't afraid of getting dirty, of doing things other folks won't. A week or two before

I even came here to these parts, I heard that the medical college in Tallahassee was looking for resurrection men and that they'd pay two hundred dollars for a cadaver. Two hundred whole dollars! *Oh, what I could do with that money*, I thought. I could get a motor carriage. I could grow my business. And then I met you, Sarah. I couldn't stop thinking about you, 'bout all the things I could do for you with the money, for us." East was nearly finished, his eyes softer than before. "So when this Cools fella kicked it, it was like I ain't have a choice. I dug him up and turned him in."

I felt sorry for East and hated him at the same time. He was a fool. He thought he had to buy Sarah with money when her affection for him had been rich enough to win her.

He held his hand out toward Sarah. "So, will you marry me?"

Zora leaped across the kitchen at East, but before she had a chance to strike him, Bob pulled her away. The commotion woke Everett from his nest in the front room. The little boy wandered into the melee, confused, sleep crusting the ends of his eyelashes like salt crystals. Mama pulled him to her waist. Sarah pounded her fist on the table. The stacks of dishes and platters jumped and we all startled.

"If you came here for the first time right now,"
Sarah said, "with my mother just buried in that same
cemetery where Chester Cools was lying, would
you have dug her up and sold her?" East opened his
mouth to answer. Sarah held up her hand. "Stop!" she
commanded. "I already know the answer. I have no
doubt you would have sold my sweet mother's body
to butchers! And here you are, standing in my mother's house, asking me if I'll marry you! A monster! I'd
rather be struck dead this very minute and join Mama
in the grave than be the wife of a monster." Sarah
stood tall and resolute. "Rot in Hell, East. It's where
you belong."

East stepped toward Sarah, still wrapped in
shameless, impossible confidence. Bob stepped in
front of him. "You heard my sister! Get outta here!"

East ignored Bob and knelt on the floor. He
almost bared his teeth. "Not without this," he said,
and picked up the silver nail that had dropped on
the floor at some point in the confrontation. Mama's
knees buckled, and with Everett on one side and me
on the other, we caught her. Zora tried to go after
East again. Bob could barely hold her back.

"It's the one thing in this house that's mine, and
I'm taking it with me. Don't worry, Sarah," East said

flatly. "I won't bother you again." We watched East depart with the nail. He stopped at the washing barrel, picked up his hat, dusted it off, placed it on his head, and doffed it at us. The devil had impeccable manners. Bob released Zora, who bolted to the door and slammed it shut.

Pale as cotton, Sarah collapsed into a chair. Everett went to her first. Then Zora, and finally, Bob. The four of them clutched one another and wept over the mountain of their shared grief. It was the last time all of Lucy Hurston's children would be together under the same roof.

CHAPTER TWENTY-SEVEN

———◦•◦•◦———

In spite of being busier than he had ever been with Eatonville's and his church's affairs, John Hurston cut loose and found time to have affairs with women in public. The evening he brought his first woman home—a buxom lady called Mattie Andrews who was just a flutter older than Sarah—Sarah sat down straightaway and wrote a letter to her grandmother. In it, she announced that she, Zora, and Everett were coming to live with her and the rest of the Pottses in Alabama. Zora thanked Sarah for including her but refused to go. Everett didn't have a choice; his mother was dead and the woman who mothered him now was Sarah, so he obeyed her.

John Hurston could never deny his favorite child anything, but one evening Zora and I were sitting on the porch and overheard him from outside, pleading with Sarah to stay.

"That evil young nigger is gone!" he said, referring to East. "I went to where he was staying in Lake Catherine, and it ain't no hoax. He's packed up and left these parts for good. He's gone. So there's no reason for you to leave. Why you wanna go so badly, huh? Why?"

"There are too many memories here," Sarah answered. "How things are now threatens to destroy them." Her meaning was unmistakable.

"How things are now?" he asked, pretending not to understand. "How things are now, your mama gone, is why I need you more than ever."

Sarah took no prisoners: "It seems like the only one 'round here you need, Daddy, is Mattie."

The thundering slap came hard and fast. Our eyes widened, and Zora grabbed my wrist. Sarah whimpered, like a songbird that had been stoned out of a tree. A door slammed, and we weren't sure who had fled the scene. When Sarah came out on the porch, her face red, her eyes redder, we knew.

Something in John Hurston did not recover from striking Sarah. For days afterward, he hardly spoke. Mattie Andrews, however, couldn't stop yakking all over town that she was taking a room at the Hurston house as a live-in domestic.

A few days later, Sarah and Everett left. Zora could not bear to see them off at the train so bade them farewell at the front gate. A sullen and defeated John Hurston drove Sarah and Everett to the station in Maitland.

At first Mattie Andrews did actually do some housekeeping. But it wasn't long before she was focusing all her energies on simply "keeping" John Hurston.

Zora could not tolerate Mattie's presence, so she began to spend nights at my house—or at the Bakers', who had a spare room and enjoyed hosting her. Other times, she'd stay late at school and Mr. Calhoun would take her home to have supper with him and his wife. Zora spent many an evening with Joe Clarke, as well, and, of course, she read away more nights than I could count at Old Lady Bronson's. It wasn't really safe to sleep outdoors, but Zora did that, too, under the Loving Pine, convinced that the force of the tree would guard her against predators of all kinds.

It was dizzying just how quickly our lives had turned. My mother had spent most of my life leaving early for work, staying on late, and boarding with sick white folks as a nursemaid for a week or two at a time. What made it possible for her to earn that living was the fact that I could eat, sleep, and experience the love of a family at the Hurston house. But with the death of Lucy Hurston and the unraveling of the Hurston family, that home away from home no longer existed.

Folks fret and they prepare mightily for the loss of the man of the house, the breadwinner. No people anywhere have ever counted on life insurance more than the cohort of colored folks I knew. We scrimped and saved and denied ourselves niceties in the present so that our kin could have a chance at grandness in the future. We set them up to survive without us because it crushed us to think of them sharecropping a piece, or serving white folks one minute and running from them through the woods the next because something came up missing or the coffee was too hot. But there is no insurance against a family losing their soul. There is no insurance against the loosening of the ties that bind and their withering in the cold wind.

If John Hurston had died, the family would have been forced to make sacrifices. Sarah would have had to work. Bob would have had to send money home; furniture would have been sold. But the family would have remained together. The family would have remained intact, unified in their love. Though John Hurston had learned how to support a family, that didn't make him a family man. Because he had wandering dust in his gut instead of roots, the family disintegrated. Ahead of schedule, Zora had to go out in the world and start becoming who she was meant to be. But, dear Lord, it was not a cakewalk. It was a trial by fire.

After school one afternoon, I accompanied Zora home. We had planned on finishing Kipling's *Kim* under the Loving Pine, but she had left the novel back at the house. It had been a month of Sundays since either of us had cracked it open. It also had been a long while since I had greased her scalp and brushed and braided her hair. I still wore a glove on my left

hand, but both sets of my fingertips were hungry
for the feel of hair besides my own to sculpt, handle, and care for. After months of upheaval and pain,
we yearned for the normalcy of a book and a hairdo.
One thing, among so many that sadden me, is that we
didn't get to finish the book that day at the Loving
Pine. We never would.

From as far as a quarter mile from the front gate,
Zora would decide whether she was going home. If
she spied her father's automobile, she'd stay away. If
it was gone, John was out. Mattie, too, trailing John
Hurston to keep his roving eye still. In which case,
Zora'd see to her errands in the house and leave. On
this day, the horseless gone, we sprinted our last leg of
the journey to fetch the book from the house. Though
it was warm, it was still winter and we wanted to soak
up as much of the crisp afternoon light as possible.
The house was perfectly quiet. Zora checked the cab-
inet under the window seat for the book; it wasn't
there. We went to the bedroom she had once shared
with Sarah and searched under the bed and on the
shelf: nothing. I went to the dining room and looked
around the buffets. Zora even hunted for it under
the table. Dust bunnies, nothing more. So much for
Mattie Andrews's housekeeping.

Finally, Zora said, "It must be in Mama's room."
I nodded and Zora darted off. The next thing I knew,
Zora was screaming. "HOW DARE YOU! HOW
DARE YOU!"

I hurried to the bedroom, where I found Zora
pulling Mattie Andrews out of her mother's feather
bed by the hair. Mattie yelped, her eyes stretched to
slits, and attempted to free herself from Zora's grip.
Mattie's bottom hit the floor, and she still hadn't
gotten loose from Zora. I got out of the way. Zora
dragged the squirming woman past me, out of her
mother's bedroom, and into the foyer.

"AND YOU'RE IN YOUR STREET
CLOTHES!" Zora screamed. "IN MAMA'S BED
IN YOUR DIRTY STREET CLOTHES!" Mattie
managed to grab one of Zora's ankles. Zora lost her
balance and, in an effort to break her fall, released
Mattie's hair. Mattie tried to stand, but the tangle of
sheets around her feet snared her. Zora pounced at the
opportunity. She straddled Mattie and slapped her in
the face, once, twice. Then Zora put her hands around
Mattie's neck and began to choke her. That's when
I finally found my wits. I leaped toward the two and
tried to pull Zora off of Mattie. Will and wild grief
had made Zora more solid than that damned well cap.

"STOP! YOU'LL KILL HER!" I shouted.

THUMP, THUMP, THUMP! Three gaveling thuds stopped my heart. I turned. It was Mr. Ambrose, banging his cane on the floor. I rocked backward, letting Zora go.

"Leave that woman be!" he commanded. "Zora, you leave her be!"

It took a moment before Zora could even register his presence, let alone his words. "Zora!" I said, bending to pull her hands away from Mattie's throat. "She's not worth all this, and you know it."

Zora stopped strangling Mattie but didn't completely release her throat or get off of her. Mattie gasped for air and began to cry.

Mr. Ambrose touched Zora on the shoulder. "Come on, now," he coaxed. "Stand up for me."

"But Mama's bed," Zora keened, her spirit in shards. "The place we were born. The place I was born. The place Mama died. She made filthy my mama's bed."

"Snidlets," Mr. Ambrose said, "this gal can't do no such thing. You know better than that."

Mr. Ambrose rapped his cane on the floor again a single time. Zora rose now, stepped away from Mattie, only to fall into Mr. Ambrose's ancient arms. He held my friend the way a father should hold a daughter, with love, tenderness, and forgiveness. Mattie scrambled to her feet, ran from the foyer, and clear out the front door.

"I'm gonna help you outta this here fix," Mr. Ambrose told Zora. I'm gonna help you git what you deserve in this life. Do you hear me, Zora Neale?"

"Yes," Zora answered, her voice surprisingly clear. "I hear you."

CHAPTER TWENTY-EIGHT

John Hurston put Zora out for good for nearly murdering the woman he said he was going to make his wife, though he never did make good on that promise.

Zora stayed with Mr. and Mrs. Calhoun for the few days it took for Mr. Ambrose to arrange for Zora to attend boarding school in Jacksonville. The girl who had feared she wouldn't be able to attend high school at all was heading for high school six months early. This was a new and big beginning for Zora. For me, it felt like a dreaded ending, almost the end of my world.

Seven years earlier, when my father didn't return home from seasonal work like he was supposed to, the days became defined by that missing piece, by his absence. The loss of my father taught me that sometimes our loved ones disappear. I understood that Zora wasn't dying, but what her life would be like in Jacksonville, a real city, one hundred forty miles away, I hadn't one clue. What did exist for me was the very real likelihood that I might never see her again.

Zora's last days in Eatonville were a flurry of nice meals and parting gifts. Mr. Calhoun cooked, which was very rare for men then, and he made his special for us: stewed chicken and dumplings. I set the table while Mrs. Calhoun took Zora's measurements in the front room. The schoolmaster's wife and my mother had a plan. Mrs. Calhoun was going to purchase Zora two store-bought dresses and have them sent to the school. Receiving something nice in the mail would buttress Zora's reputation among the girls, Mrs. Calhoun thought. Meanwhile Mama prepared an excellent sewing kit for Zora to take with her, complete with a rainbow of threads, needles with eyes enough to get a rich man into Heaven, fabric for nice patches, and, of course, ribbon.

Mrs. Calhoun freed my friend from the chain of

her tape measure. "I'm done, Zora." But getting fussed over was a gilded cage Zora seemed to be warming to.

"Mrs. Calhoun," she asked, "what colors do you think best suit me?"

Mrs. Calhoun smiled. "All of them. What colors do you prefer?"

Zora pondered the question, the answer to which was suddenly and surprisingly important. For Zora, who had eschewed appearances all her life, a burgeoning interest in clothes wasn't about showing off. It was about revealing the color and tone of what she felt.

"Pale purple," Zora answered. "And ivory."

"I'll be sure to remember that," Mrs. Calhoun said as Mr. Calhoun stepped into the dining room with the bowl of stew, placed it in the center of the table beside a pitcher of grapefruit punch, then untied his apron and draped it over a chair.

"Time to eat," he announced. We all took our seats.

"Bless the bounty of my husband's hands," Mrs. Calhoun prayed, "that it may nourish these two girls you have granted us the favor of welcoming into our home. Please, Lord, keep Zora safe in body and mind at school in Jacksonville and bring her home again to us all very, very soon. Amen."

Mr. Calhoun said amen, and I did, too. Zora sat silent.

"You all right?" Mr. Calhoun lifted the bowl of chicken and dumplings and passed it to Zora. Zora passed it on to Mrs. Calhoun without serving herself. Mrs. Calhoun spooned a fluffy dumpling and some brown meat and gravy onto Zora's plate anyways. Sadness had stripped away Zora's appetite, as it had mine, I realized.

"Mr. Calhoun," Zora answered, "I'm grateful that I've been enrolled in school in Jacksonville. But I can't help thinking that I got what I most wanted in the world because Mama died. Mama died!" Zora erupted into sobs, the dam of her grief broken by a flood of guilt.

Mr. Calhoun looked at Zora with compassion and understanding. Folks are like locked chests. You can't guess which key will open the lid on their experience, especially when you're a child. Yet that's just where the key to most reside: their childhoods.

"Coping with grief isn't about feeling better," Mr. Calhoun said. "It's about not feeling alone in your grief." As he said this, Mrs. Calhoun gazed at the man with whom she had built a happy life. A life, I intimated, that was not free from any kind of agony.

"My mama died when I was a little older than you," Mr. Calhoun continued. "Afterward, some of her friends — all domestics — pooled portions of their savings and sent me to college in Pennsylvania. They gave me my start in the world. Those women let me know I wasn't alone. Neither are you, Zora. You're not alone with this."

Zora replied, "But I will be in Jacksonville."

"No, you won't," I jumped in, hoping against hope that I could stop my own heart from breaking. "Every night, I'll sit down and write to tell you everything that's happening here. It will feel like you've never left Eatonville. And you'll do the same: You'll write and tell me all 'bout Jacksonville, the school, the other girls, and your classes. Why, you'll make it feel like I'm right there with you! We'll only ever be a letter away from each other and neither of us will feel alone." Everyone nodded and agreed and wiped tears, and we went on eating our chicken and dumpling stew, but I'm not sure I had managed to convince anyone, least of all Zora and myself.

I hardly slept the night before Zora was set to catch the train for Jacksonville. The morning of her departure, I could hardly stop crying. I couldn't bear to see

Zora go, though she had to. Zora would always have Eatonville in her heart, but it was no longer home for her.

Well-wishers gathered at the Calhoun house to say goodbye. The Calhouns, the Bakers, Mr. Clarke, Mama, and Old Lady Bronson drank coffee on the porch. Mr. Ambrose had offered to drive Zora to the station but hadn't yet arrived. Teddy and I sat with Zora in the front room to sulk. "The streets in Jacksonville will be so busy," I said in a dull attempt to make conversation. "Do be careful, Zora." In Eatonville, everyone knew Zora. In Jacksonville, I was keenly aware, no one would. Anonymity could free white men from the consequences of their actions. Anonymity transformed women, coloreds, and especially colored women into prey.

"Carrie," Teddy countered, "don't forget that our hometown isn't exactly the paragon of safety. It's a place where there's been a grave robbery, not to mention a murder, and an attempted murder. I think Eatonville has prepared Zora to handle herself in the big city just fine."

Zora, who had been uncomfortably silent all morning, gave a little chuckle. Then another and another, until a full-on belly laugh filled the room with buoyancy enough to float Zora to Jacksonville. Teddy joined in. I wanted to laugh, too, and I was relieved that Zora could find it in herself to laugh at all. But I couldn't. Teddy had reminded me of the litany of evil things that occurred in Eatonville. To me, Zora leaving was one more.

"What you three in here hooting and hollering 'bout?" Mr. Baker boomed as he came into the front room, holding a cup of coffee.

Zora said, "Your son here just made the case for how Eatonville has prepared me to survive in the big, scary world. It wasn't pretty."

"Leave it to a future doctor to frighten the bejesus out of someone." Mr. Baker held the screen door open for us as we filed out onto the porch in order to say our proper goodbyes.

Mr. Calhoun addressed all three of us when he said, "You are well prepared to attend any high school in this state. You're graduates of one of the best one-room schoolhouses in Florida. Every grown-up on that porch beamed proudly, like they were each a parent to every one of us. "For our people," Mr. Calhoun continued, "there may be nothing more important than a formal education. At the same time, you have learned a great many lessons outside of my classroom.

A lot of those lessons have been ugly, but they will be as valuable to you as your book learning."

"Sometimes more valuable," Old Lady Bronson added. "I have a gift for you, Zora." She reached deep into one of her giant apron pockets and pulled out a book. She handed it to Zora, who registered its weight in her palm. The title and the name of the author were embossed on the black cover in gold. Zora traced the lettering with her finger like it was the route on a treasure map. "*History of Brazil, Volume I,* by Robert Southey," Zora read out loud.

"In that book," the old lady said, "you'll discover how and when the word *zombie* came into the English language — and even how the idea of zombies has survived to this day."

Zora put the book to her chest and closed her eyes, as if allowing it to read her heart. Then she embraced the old woman.

"Take it from someone who knows," Old Lady Bronson said, squeezing Zora tight. "Some folks will try to take down and cast out a woman with a past. But I'm here to tell you that a woman with a past is a woman who has not let life pass her by. A woman with a past is a woman who has lived and dared and risked. And that's the only kind of woman who can become immortal. So keep on living and daring and risking, Zora. Don't let anyone take you down. Maybe you will achieve immortality yourself."

Mr. Ambrose's horseless was approaching, which prompted Joe Clarke to chime in, "Lucia's not the only one who has something for you." He sprang down the stairs and knelt to retrieve something that was just out of sight. Mr. Clarke stood up, holding a beautiful pollard oak lap desk. He carried it back onto the porch and held it out to Zora. Zora ran her hand across the sloped writing surface. At the center, there was a large diamond shape inlaid with mother-of-pearl, and in the center of the diamond, a small circle inlaid with black onyx. She raised the lid of the desk. Inside she discovered paper, pens, and two corked crystal bottles for ink. Zora smiled more brightly than she had for months.

"Do you like it?" Joe asked.

"Oh, Mr. Clarke, it's the most beautiful thing I've ever seen! I love it! Thank you." Zora put her arms around Joe Clarke's neck and kissed him on the cheek.

"You'll be fine," Joe murmured, still holding the desk in his arms. "You will."

By this time, Mr. Ambrose had parked his horseless. "Well, Snidlets," he called from the driver's seat,

"I think it's time we go. You've got a train to catch."

Mama went inside and retrieved Zora's one small suitcase for her. "You have your sewing kit in here, don't you?" she asked.

"Yes," Zora said. "I packed it last night. Thank you." Zora opened the suitcase and placed the book from Old Lady Bronson and the lap desk on top of her things, then closed it again. They both fit easily.

Mama touched Zora's shoulder, then came to her senses and pulled her in for a proper embrace. "Take care now, you hear? A mended sleeve can sometimes stand in for a mended heart."

"Yes, ma'am."

Mrs. Baker was next. "Just be yourself, girl, and you'll climb high in the world," she foretold, "mighty high."

Mr. Baker patted Zora on the back and nodded.

The Calhouns embraced Zora together. "It's been an honor to be your teacher," Mr. Calhoun said. "Never stop being a student of the world, Zora. Never."

"I won't," Zora answered. "Thank you both for everything."

Old Lady Bronson kissed Zora on the forehead. "The world's a harsh teacher, as you know. So be kind to yourself. That example will give others a lesson in how they should treat you."

"I love you all," Zora said.

Teddy opened the passenger-side door of the horseless, and Zora climbed in. Mama slid Zora's suitcase into the back seat of the automobile. They were all set to go, but Mr. Ambrose was looking all around the car, like something was missing. Finally, he glared at me and Teddy. "You mean to say that you two aren't coming to the station?"

Mr. Baker guffawed, then cried, "Of course they are!" and shooed us toward the car. "Go on, you two!" everyone called, laughing, waving us along. So Teddy climbed into the back next to the suitcase and I piled in beside Zora. Mr. Ambrose started the engine, and we pulled away.

The ride to the station felt long because I could feel myself already missing Zora. I could already feel the miles stretching between us.

At the station, I got out first. Teddy climbed out next, holding Zora's suitcase. Zora slid over to get out, too, but before she did, Mr. Ambrose placed an envelope in her hands.

"What's this?" she asked.

"Your ticket," he answered, "and a little something

besides to pick up a book or some candy when you feel like it."

The two shared a kindly embrace and then Zora got out of the car. "Aren't you coming with us to the platform?" she asked. Mr. Ambrose hadn't moved from the driver's seat.

"I think the job of seeing you off is covered."

"I can't tell you how much I appreciate everything you've done," Zora said.

"Well, you've lucked out, Snidlets. You don't have to. Go on, now. I hear the train."

"I hear it, too," Teddy said.

The train whistle blew and the sound of it unnerved me. The three of us hustled over to the platform, where a few folks already stood waiting. Zora removed the ticket and the money from the envelope and quickly slipped the bills down into one of her socks. The train bellowed into the station in a plume of smoke and steam.

The train screeched to a long, slow stop, and a mustachioed conductor disembarked. He wore a black hat and a dark jacket with two rows of sparkling gold buttons running down the front. He popped open a silver pocket watch. It seemed to glow, even in broad daylight, like a full moon. The man blazoned, "All aboard! All aboard! Eight forty-two to Jacksonville. All aboard!"

"I guess this is it." Zora reached for her suitcase.

"I guess it is," Teddy said, giving her a hug. "I'll miss you," he said with a sniffle.

"I'll miss you, too."

Then Zora turned to me. Her eyes filled and then spilled over. "Take good care of him, Carrie. And of yourself and Eatonville." Her voice broke. "I'll write as much as I can. I promise."

The conductor walked toward us. "Tickets, please." Zora handed him the slip of paper. "Welcome aboard," he said to her, then pointed to the car at the rear of the train.

I threw my arms around Zora. "I love you," I said. "You've meant everything to me and you always will."

"I love you, Carrie."

We watched Zora walk away from us, down the length of the train, all the way to the last car. There, she turned back to wave, then climbed the steps and disappeared. A moment later, the train pulled out, slowly at first, then faster and faster. Finally came the last car. We looked up and saw Zora, filling a window, waving and waving. Teddy and I waved back. We waved until we could no longer see the train.

Long after the locomotive and its smoke and steam had vanished, Teddy and I still stood by the tracks, hand in hand, gazing at the empty horizon.

I could already feel time moving differently. Once Zora found her place in this world, everyone and everything in it would have to start moving a little faster just to catch up.

EPILOGUE

The months that followed Zora's departure from Eatonville revealed a new perspective on the death of Chester Cools and on Teddy's illness. Turns out that it may not have been a heart attack that killed Chester Cools but a fever, an illness, that got passed on to Teddy when Teddy helped Doc Brazzle prepare Mr. Cools's body. In downtown Tallahassee, a few folks connected with the medical school came up sick, then a few more. Their symptoms all sounded a lot like Teddy's. Because East had told us the ghastly truth about the fate of Chester Cools, it didn't take long for us to put the pieces of the puzzle together. We all knew for sure now where the old man's body had taken up final, grisly residence.

White folks, on the other hand, were wringing their hands, wondering if God was delivering retribution on Eatonville's behalf for the lynching of Terrace Side and the desecration of a grave that may or may not have belonged to a zombie. Joe Clarke's proposal to expand our town had languished in the halls of state government for years, but Tallahassee was ready to wager that they could end their blight by giving us, the Negroes, permission to build a bigger town. The expansion wasn't Mr. Clarke's idea anymore. It was simply a good idea. Nevertheless, John Hurston sopped up all the credit for the turn in our fortunes, while he blithely shook off accountability in his private life.

Zora had been living in Jacksonville for a year when Mr. Ambrose, who had been paying her school bills, died. The school began sending the bills to her father. John Hurston refused to pay. For a while, the school put Zora to work to cover her room and board, then they ran out of enough things for her to do to cover the costs. So then she took on a domestic job in Jacksonville to pay for school herself. With less time on her hands, Zora wrote to me less. Then her letters stopped altogether. Eventually my letters to her were returned, unopened. Zora had left school. Many years passed before I heard from Zora again or had any idea where she had gone.

It wasn't until she was a student again, at the famed Howard University in Washington, DC, that Zora renewed our correspondence. She filled me in on the missing years: She had worked as a maid for a beautiful, temperamental actress in a traveling theater company. More exotic yet, for a short time, she had been a domestic for the lady acrobats of a struggling circus. She confessed to having lied about her age in order to be allowed to finish high school in Maryland. In all the years I knew her growing up here in Eatonville, Zora had turned exaggeration into an art, but to the best of my knowledge, she never outright lied. In the larger world, it looked like lying was somewhat necessary for survival. I've since learned, of course, that she was not alone in that. Most women who got ahead then, who had ambition, likely had to do a fair bit of lying.

A southern soul determined to become a northern star, after Howard University, Zora dropped anchor in New York City as a student at Barnard College. During that period, I stalked the post office in Atlanta where Teddy and I lived at the time, eager for one of Zora's glorious updates detailing gin parties, rent parties, and book parties. She'd send news of friends, copies of her publications, and pictures of herself wearing stylish hats, dressed in long dresses, and draped to her waist in beads.

As for Teddy and me, Teddy followed in Doc Brazzle's footsteps, enrolling at the Meharry Medical College. I enrolled in the nursing program there and we had been married two years when I had my first baby. Alexander, your father, was born a month after I graduated. Teddy completed his residency in Atlanta where there were a whopping two colored hospitals. We stayed on there for many years with Alexander and your aunt Rebecca.

One day, early in October, I was helping Teddy by delivering medicine to a patient. It was late afternoon, and Rebecca, who must have been four at the time, was with me. The neighborhood was entirely unfamiliar to me; it was lovely, old. Walking down that nice street, lined with big houses on that golden October afternoon, I got a chill. I was scared without knowing why. I must have been gripping Rebecca's little hand hard because she squealed in pain and pulled away. Her reaction made me stop and try to

get my bearings. I looked up to see that I was standing in front of a familiar house. The fence, the eaves,
the porch, the ancient sycamore. I had seen this very
house before, all those years ago in the pictures from
Mr. Cools's trunk.

I never did deliver the medicine, and I never went
to that neighborhood again.

When things began to go bad up north for
Zora—publishing troubles, folks saying mean and
vicious things about what she wrote, crazy neighbors accusing her of things that made her sick in the
heart—it took Zora an awfully long time to come
back home, where she could be loved, where she could
heal. Too long, and I had a hard time forgiving her
for that.

As fate would have it, Zora and I were bookends
in each other's lives. Girls together, we got to be old
ladies together, too. Unable to gallivant through the
dim forest like we used to, we sat instead in dark the-
aters and watched movies about what America thought
it was and what America aspired to be. Arthritic and
heavyset, we gave up swimming and fished instead. On
porches, we ate ice cream and read aloud, hearing our
own thoughts and feelings and experiences echoed in
every web of story we explored. And in my own time,

in my own space, I read every single thing that Zora wrote. It was a mirror on the world that raised me, a window on the soul of my best friend, a testament to a mind and a person born ahead of her time. My sincere hope is that, somewhere in these pages, you catch a glimpse of who you are and where you come from, and the web of stories to which you will add your own brightly gleaming threads. Zora would love that. More than anything in this world, I would love that, too.

ZORA NEALE HURSTON

A Biography

To hear Zora Neale Hurston tell it, she was born in Eatonville, Florida, the daughter of a mayor, in 1901, or 1903, or 1910. Even from a young age, Hurston was an inventor of stories, a creator of masks and disguises. In reality, she was born in 1891 in Notasulga, Alabama, the fifth of eight children raised by John and Lucy Hurston. Her mother was a schoolteacher and her father, born into slavery, a carpenter and preacher (who did eventually become the mayor of Eatonville).

Although Alabama was her place of birth, Eatonville, Florida, was the place that truly felt like home to Zora. It was the first incorporated all-black township in the United States, established by twenty-seven African-American men soon after the Emancipation Proclamation. Hurston and her family moved to Eatonville when she was just a toddler, and the thriving community infected her with energy, confidence, and ambition. Hurston's childhood was idyllic.

But then in 1904, when Hurston was just thirteen, her mother passed away. Thus began what Zora would later call the "haunted years." Lucy Hurston had been the one to encourage her daughter to have courageous dreams. John Hurston encouraged his daughter, too, but just as often tried to tame her rambunctious spirit, sometimes harshly. After his wife died, John had little energy or money to devote to his children and grew detached from them emotionally. When he remarried, his new wife and Zora were like oil and water.

Zora left home after a vicious fight with the new Mrs. Hurston and struggled to finish high school while working a variety of different jobs. One of those jobs was working as a maid to a singer in a traveling theater troupe, an experience that sparked Hurston's love of performance, a passion that would last the rest of her life. In 1917, she found herself in Baltimore. She was twenty-six and still without her high-school diploma. So Hurston lied about her age, convincing the school that she was sixteen so that she could re-enroll and complete her education. From that point on, Hurston would always present herself as younger than she actually was.

In 1919, Hurston entered college, first at Howard University and then at Barnard College, where she was the only black student and studied under the famous anthropologist Franz Boas. During these years, her writing began to get recognized. Her first short story, "John Redding Goes to Sea," was published in Howard University's literary magazine in 1921.

In the 1920s, Hurston moved to New York City and became an integral part of the Harlem Renaissance, befriending poet Langston Hughes and singer-actress Ethel Waters, among many other cultural luminaries. Zora was the life of the party, frequently hosting artists at her home (though she retreated into her room when she needed to get any writing done).

In 1933, publisher Bertram Lippincott read Hurston's short story "The Gilded Six-Bits" and inquired as to whether she might be working on a novel. Hurston answered yes — and then set to work writing one, which became *Jonah's Gourd Vine*. By 1935, Hurston had her first novel and a collection of southern folktales under her publishing belt.

In 1936, the travel dust that Hurston's mother thought must have been sprinkled in her shoes allowed her to leave the shores of North America. After applying for and receiving a Guggenheim Fellowship, she traveled to Haiti on the island of Hispaniola and to Jamaica to study indigenous religious practices. In both places, she was a keen observer as well as a full participant in *vodoun* practices.

In 1937, Hurston's most renowned novel, *Their Eyes Were Watching God*, was published. In that novel, Hurston's heroine, Janie Crawford, lives a conventionally circumscribed life until she chooses to break out of the mold and live only for herself. Much like Hurston, Janie has her eyes on the horizon and believes in a better life beyond it. The novel has been praised as a classic of black literature and a tribute to the strength of black women.

Hurston went on to write several other works, including a study of Caribbean voodoo practices, two more novels, and her autobiography, *Dust Tracks on a Road*. All in all, she wrote four novels and more than fifty short stories, plays, and essays. Sadly, Hurston never enjoyed any monetary reward for her success during her lifetime. When she died in 1960 at the age of sixty-nine, her neighbors had to take up a collection for the funeral. Hurston was buried in an unmarked grave in Fort Pierce, Florida, because the neighbors hadn't been able to raise enough funds for a funeral *and* a gravestone.

In 1973, a young writer named Alice Walker traveled to Fort Pierce to visit the burial site of the woman who had inspired so many black female authors with her courage and strength: Hurston had insisted on living life on her own terms during a time when most women, and especially black women, had few professional options. "A people do not forget their geniuses," Walker said, and arranged to have a monument placed, at last, to honor the life and achievements of Zora Neale Hurston.

A Time Line of Zora Neale Hurston's Life

1891
Born in Notasulga, Alabama, the fifth of eight
children, to John Hurston, a carpenter and preacher,
and Lucy Potts Hurston, a former schoolteacher.

1894
The Hurston family moves to Eatonville, Florida,
a small all-black community.

1897
Hurston's father is elected mayor of Eatonville.

1904
Lucy Potts Hurston dies.

1917–1918
Attends Morgan Academy in Baltimore, Maryland,
and completes high-school requirements.

1918
Works as a waitress at a nightclub and a manicurist
at a barbershop that serves only whites.

1919–1924
Attends Howard University and receives an associate
degree.

1921
Publishes her first story, "John Redding Goes to Sea," in Howard University's literary magazine.

1925–1927
Moves to New York City and attends Barnard College as its only black student. Receives a bachelor of arts degree.

1927
Goes to Florida to collect folktales.

1927
Marries Herbert Sheen.

1930–1932
Organizes the field notes that become *Mules and Men*.

1930
Works on the play *Mule Bone* with Langston Hughes.

1931
Breaks with Langston Hughes over the authorship of *Mule Bone*.

1931
Divorces Sheen.

1934
Publishes *Jonah's Gourd Vine*, her first novel.

1935
Mules and Men, a collection of folklore, is published.

1936
Awarded a Guggenheim Fellowship to study West Indian *obeah* practices. Travels to Jamaica and Haiti. While in Haiti, she writes *Their Eyes Were Watching God* in seven weeks.

1937
Their Eyes Were Watching God is published.

1938
Tell My Horse is published.

1939
Receives an honorary doctor of letters degree from Morgan State College.

1939
Marries Albert Price III. They are later divorced.

1939
Moses, Man of the Mountain is published.

ZORA NEALE HURSTON

An Annotated Bibliography

The Complete Stories (1995)

Published after her death, this collection features Zora Neale Hurston's short fiction, which was originally published in literary magazines during her lifetime. Spanning Hurston's writing career from 1921 to 1955, the compilation showcases the writer's range, rich language, and development as a storyteller.

Dust Tracks on a Road (1942)

Hurston's autobiography tells the story of her rise from poverty to literary prominence. The writer's story is told with imagination and exuberance and offers a glimpse into the life of one of America's most esteemed writers.

Every Tongue Got to Confess: Negro Folk-Tales from the Gulf States (2001)

Originally collected by Hurston in 1927, this volume of folklore passed down through generations offers

1942
Hurston's autobiography, *Dust Tracks on a Road*,
is published.

1947
Goes to British Honduras to research black
communities and writes *Seraph on the Suwanee.*

1948
Seraph on the Suwanee is published.

1956
Works as a librarian at Patrick Air Force Base,
Florida.

1958
Works as a substitute teacher at Lincoln Park
Academy in Fort Pierce, Florida.

1959
Suffers a stroke and enters the St. Lucie County
Welfare Home.

1960
Dies in the St. Lucie County Welfare Home.
Buried in an unmarked grave in Fort Pierce.

a glimpse of the African American experience in the South at the turn of the century.

Jonah's Gourd Vine (1934)
Hurston's first published novel. Based loosely on her parents' lives, it features a preacher and his wife as the main characters.

Moses, Man of the Mountain (1939)
An allegory based on the story of the Exodus and blending the Moses of the Old Testament with the Moses of black folklore and song. Narrated in a mixture of biblical rhetoric, black dialect, and colloquial English.

Mule Bone: A Comedy of Negro Life (1930)
A collaboration between Hurston and Langston Hughes, this comedic play is set in Eatonville, Florida, and focuses on the lives of two men and the woman who comes between them. Due to a copyright disagreement between Hurston and Hughes, the play was not performed until 1991.

Mules and Men (1935)
Gathered by Hurston in the 1930s, the first great

collection of black America's folk world, including oral histories, sermons, and songs, some dating as far back as the Civil War.

Seraph on the Suwanee (1948)
A novel that explores the nature of love, faith, and marriage set at the turn of the century among white "Florida Crackers."

Tell My Horse: Voodoo and Life in Haiti and Jamaica (1938)
Hurston's travelogue of her time spent in Haiti and Jamaica in the 1930s practicing and learning about voodoo ceremonies, customs, and superstitions.

Their Eyes Were Watching God (1937)
The most widely read and highly acclaimed novel in African American literature and the piece of writing for which Zora Neale Hurston is best known. Tells the story of Janie Crawford as she develops a sense of self through three marriages and grows into an independent woman.

Children's Books Adapted from Folktales Collected by Zora Neale Hurston

Lies and Other Tall Tales. Adapted and illustrated by Christopher Myers. New York: HarperCollins, 2005.

The Six Fools. Adapted by Joyce Carol Thomas. Illustrated by Ann Tanksley. New York: HarperCollins, 2005.

The Skull Talks Back and Other Haunting Tales. Adapted by Joyce Carol Thomas. Illustrated by Leonard Jenkins. New York: HarperCollins, 2004.

The Three Witches. Adapted by Joyce Carol Thomas. Illustrated by Faith Ringgold. New York: HarperCollins, 2006.

What's the Hurry, Fox? and Other Animal Stories. Adapted by Joyce Carol Thomas. Illustrated by Bryan Collier. New York: HarperCollins, 2004.

ACKNOWLEDGMENTS

Now and always, thank you to my husband, Drew Baughman. You made this book possible with your love and insight. Thank you as well to friends who, over the course of nearly five years, read drafts and supported and encouraged me: Allison Pease, Christen Madrazo, Yasmin Dalisay, Charles Davidson, and Dianne Rodgers. To T. R. Simon, thank you for inviting me to cocreate this series; I will always be grateful for your generosity. Thank you to Sarah Haley: your scholarship and dedication to justice inspired so much in this book. To Lucy Hurston, Zora's niece: your blessing from the start has been good juju. And to my editor, Mary Lee Donovan: There is no way that I can ever repay the debt I owe you. At every turn, you guided my imagination and my pen to something better, something clearer, something truer. To Andrea Tompa: you have my gratitude for your thoughtfulness, especially about character motivations as the key to a sound story. To my grandparents, Charles and Dolores Biot, who have helped to author my life, I will always be grateful to you for my love of stories, history, and the life of the mind. And thank you to Zora Neale Hurston herself, whose life and work, a testament to the beauty, brilliance, and struggle of the African American experience, continues to inspire.